THE PHILADELPHIA ADVENTURE

OTHER YEARLING BOOKS BY LLOYD ALEXANDER YOU WILL ENJOY:

THE ILLYRIAN ADVENTURE

THE EL DORADO ADVENTURE

THE DRACKENBERG ADVENTURE

THE JEDERA ADVENTURE

THE BOOK OF THREE

THE BLACK CAULDRON

THE CASTLE OF LLYR

TARAN WANDERER

THE HIGH KING

TIME CAT

YEARLING BOOKS/YOUNG YEARLINGS/YEARLING CLASSICS are designed especially to entertain and enlighten young people. Patricia Reilly Giff, consultant to this series, received her bachelor's degree from Marymount College and a master's degree in history from St. John's University. She holds a Professional Diploma in Reading and a Doctorate of Humane Letters from Hofstra University. She was a teacher and reading consultant for many years, and is the author of numerous books for young readers.

For a complete listing of all Yearling titles, write to Dell Readers Service, P.O. Box 1045, South Holland, IL 60473.

THE PHILADELPHIA
ADVENTURE

Lloyd Alexander

A Yearling Book

Published by
Dell Publishing
a division of
Bantam Doubleday Dell Publishing Group, Inc.
666 Fifth Avenue
New York, New York 10103

The trademark Yearling® is registered in the U.S. Patent and Trademark Office.

The trademark Dell® is registered in the U.S. Patent and Trademark Office.

ISBN: 0-440-40605-6

Reprinted by arrangement with Dutton Children's Books, a division of Penguin Books USA Inc.

Printed in the United States of America

April 1992

10 9 8 7 6 5 4 3 2 1

OPM

for voyagers ending one adventure
to begin another

THE PHILADELPHIA
ADVENTURE

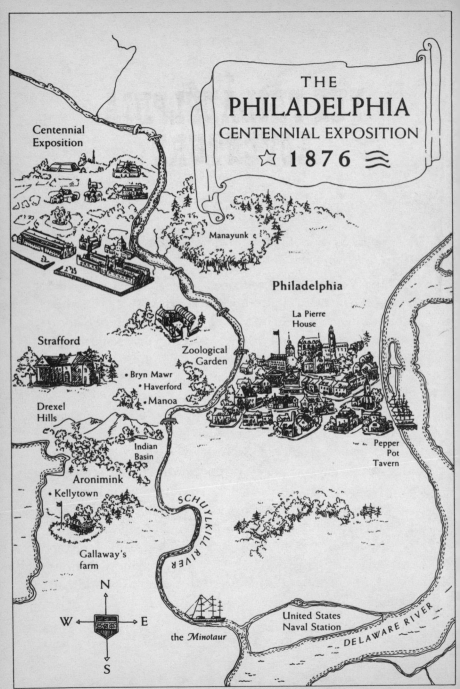

THE
PHILADELPHIA
CENTENNIAL EXPOSITION
☆ 1876 ≋

Centennial Exposition

Manayunk

Philadelphia

La Pierre House

Strafford

Zoological Garden

• Bryn Mawr
• Haverford
• Manoa

Drexel Hills

Indian Basin

Pepper Pot Tavern

Aronimink

• Kellytown

SCHUYLKILL RIVER

Gallaway's farm

N
W — E
S

the *Minotaur*

United States Naval Station

DELAWARE RIVER

Map by Debby L. Carter

1

Miss Vesper Holly welcomes visitors, even uninvited ones. So, on a warm afternoon early in May 1876, when the president of the United States appeared on her doorstep, she behaved with true Philadelphia grace and hospitality. In some ways, I am sorry that she did.

Until that fateful moment, we had been enjoying glasses of lemonade in the drawing room of Vesper's Strafford mansion: my wife, Mary, and I, Professor Brinton Garrett; Smiler and Slider, who had become sturdy additions to the household since our return from North Africa; and Vesper, comfortably sprawled in an armchair with Moggie, her big orange cat, occupying her lap.

Vesper had been outlining plans for us to visit the Centennial Exposition. I prefer my beekeeping and my studies in Etruscan history to clanking machinery. Still, I recognized that the Exposition promised to be the most glorious display of scientific and industrial wonders the world had seen.

"It will be." Vesper sipped her lemonade. "If it ever opens."

True, the great event had been plagued by constant, often mysterious postponements. However, I pointed out, in an enterprise of this magnitude—over two hundred acres of our city's magnificent Fairmount Park, some fifty nations exhibiting their achievements, an expected public attendance of ten million, as well as countless domestic and foreign dignitaries—such delays were to be expected. France, for example, had sent the arm of the Statue of Liberty but had just recently completed assembling the upraised torch.

"The French," Mary observed, "have never been known to finish anything on time. Heaven help us if they had tried to put up the whole figure."

At that point, insistent knocking sounded at the front door. Our housekeeper was on leave to visit an ailing relative, so Smiler and Slider went to determine the cause of this interruption. They hurried back from the hallway a few moments later. The stalwart twin brothers had gone through any number of horrendous experiences with stolid courage. They were identically unflappable. Until now, I had never seen such a look of astonishment on their moon-round, weather-beaten faces.

"It's Grant," said Smiler, as if disbelieving his own words.

"Grant who?" inquired Vesper.

"Why, Miss Vesper, it's himself," said Slider. "Mr. Ulysses S. Grant."

"He wants to see you," Smiler added.

Vesper has been on familiar terms with kings, grand duchesses, blue-skinned sheiks, and Central American Indian chieftains. But the president of the United States was enough to spark her curiosity.

"Better show him in," she said.

There was no need. With the resolution and initiative that so distinguished his wartime career, President Grant had not waited for an invitation. He had already come into the drawing room, where he halted at the edge of the Turkey carpet. Beside him stood two burly, thick-necked men in black suits, with the unmistakable bulge of revolvers under their coats. They looked as cheerful as crocodiles dressed up like undertakers.

Grant, arms folded across his chest, glanced around the room, a general surveying the terrain. "Miss Vesper Holly?"

Vesper smiled cordially and acknowledged her identity. Grant seemed a little taken aback. What he expected I could not guess, but it was probably not a young woman of twenty with startlingly green eyes and marmalade-colored hair. Vesper was wearing a bright red caftan that her late father, and my dear friend, Dr. Benjamin Rittenhouse Holly, the brilliant scholar and fearless adventurer, had sent to her from Algiers. It was her favorite garment, but hardly the costume usually found in our Quaker city. A Gypsy amulet on a gold chain and a pair of Chirican Indian sandals contributed to the dazzling effect.

President Grant swallowed down whatever surprise he felt and addressed the crocodiles, "Outside. Wait in the carriage."

The two lumbered from the drawing room. When certain the door had shut behind them, Grant again turned to Vesper.

"I'm sorry to intrude, Miss Holly. I have a matter to

discuss." He sat down stiffly on the chair Vesper indicated. "An extremely urgent matter."

"Care for some lemonade?" said Vesper.

The president shook his head. Poor fellow, he looked terrible. His beard was a little scruffy, his face tight-set, his complexion pallid. Never had I seen a man so brutally burdened by the cares of high office. Understandably, in view of the rash of scandals besetting his administration through no fault of his own, and his political enemies in full cry against him. Even his starched collar appeared to be throttling him. No doubt he would have been more happily at ease in the unbuttoned army jacket and baggy trousers that Mr. Mathew Brady had immortalized in photographs.

"We must speak in privacy," Grant said. "Complete privacy," he added pointedly. "If you'd kindly ask the company here to withdraw."

"Aunt Mary and dear old Brinnie are my legal guardians. They are also my trusted friends, as are Smiler and Slider. Whatever you wish to say to me can be said in front of them."

"Miss Holly, it is a matter of extreme urgency, of national importance."

"All the more reason for them to be here."

Grant scowled. A chief of state is not used to being contradicted. But he had not known Vesper very long. She settled herself in the armchair, waiting. Finally, Grant nodded. He turned his sharp blue eyes on each of us, with a double glance at Smiler and Slider.

"You can rely on them absolutely," said Vesper. "I do."

"I guess I'll have to," said Grant, not especially pleased. "One thing understood, then. You'll keep what I tell you a total secret. I mean that. Not a word leaves this room, not a whisper. Never. Your solemn vow, all of you."

Our assurances evidently satisfied him, and as he realized, he had little choice. He blew out his breath and relaxed somewhat. Vesper does have the gift of putting people at ease, even in touchy circumstances. "I'll have some of that lemonade now."

The president leaned back in his chair. "I'll tell you this, to begin. I came to Philadelphia to inspect the arrangements for the Exposition. I'll be here again to open it officially."

"Whenever that may be," remarked Vesper.

"Wednesday next," said Grant. "The tenth of May. That's for sure."

"So the newspapers say," replied Vesper. "I wonder. First, it was going to be early April. Then late April. And now—"

"The tenth," said Grant. "Take it from me, it's a fact."

"I'm glad to hear that." Vesper refilled the glass of lemonade which the president had downed in one gulp. "But I don't think you came to talk to me about the Exposition."

"No, young lady, I didn't." Grant produced one of his notorious cigars and lit it. "I'll say, though, it's a good thing I happened to be in Philadelphia. It turns out I'm in a position to help someone I respect and admire. And do a lot more besides.

"I'm talking about a very nasty piece of business,"

Grant went on. "It has to be settled right now, double-quick. Not only for the sake of my friend. There's more to it. If so much as a hint of what's happened gets out—Well, I don't want to contemplate the results.

"We have an election coming up in the fall. I've got nothing to do with it; I won't run for a third term; they'll have to find somebody else. I've had my fill of the job, and I'm glad to be shut of it.

"We haven't even had the nominating conventions yet, but the high muckety-mucks of both parties are already at each other's throats. There's been more skulduggery, plain and fancy monkeyshines, than you'd care to imagine. And worse. The public doesn't realize—leastways, I hope not—we're sitting on a powder keg. Some hotheads are talking armed insurrection, I haven't seen anything like it since the war."

Grant leaned forward. "If certain people get wind of this affair, they'll use it to suit their purposes. The consequences—I guarantee you wouldn't like them.

"So I'm here to ask a favor. Not just for my friend. Or me. For the whole blessed United States of America."

❧ 2 ❧

When individuals of great power ask a favor, it usually involves something disagreeable, difficult, or dangerous. Even so, seeing the hero of Appomattox and chief magistrate of our noble republic looking so wretched and so clearly troubled, I could not restrain myself. What Philadelphian could? I sprang to my feet, despite Mary's tugging at my coattails and whispering at me to be quiet.

"Sir," I declared, "if there is a service any of us can perform, you have only to name it."

"Not so fast." Grant raised a hand. "The young lady here is the one to answer."

"Mr. President—" Vesper began.

"Anybody who will do me this big a favor can call me 'Sam,'" said Grant. "You'd better let me tell you about it first. Now, that friend I mentioned. He's a mighty high dignitary. High as anyone can be, I guess. He's in Philadelphia—"

"You mean the emperor of Brazil?" said Vesper. "Dom Pedro II?"

"You're quick off the mark." The president gave a grunt of approval. "I see you're well informed."

"Everybody knows," said Vesper. "Dom Pedro and Empress Theresa are staying at La Pierre House. They're traveling incognito, but Dom Pedro can't keep himself a secret. Not that he wants to. It just makes things easier for him."

Vesper, of course, meant that Dom Pedro's pretending to be an ordinary visitor was merely a diplomatic pretext. It relieved him of the formal obligations he could not have escaped in his official capacity.

"I gather from what I've read," Vesper added, "that you and Dom Pedro are supposed to open the Exposition."

"Correct." Grant nodded. "We'll both be there to start it off. His Majesty's also brought a couple of youngsters with him, children of his close friends in Brazil. They're doing a little sight-seeing."

"How lovely," said Mary. "What a treat for them. They will surely benefit from the experience. The exposure to our historical monuments: Independence Hall, the Liberty Bell—"

"Yes, all of that," said Grant. "They've been having a fine time. Until now."

"Have they fallen ill?" Mary said anxiously. "I pray not."

If that were the case, I hastened to assure the president that our advanced medical facilities, our superbly skilled physicians and diagnosticians were unrivaled in the world.

Whatever their malady, our honored young visitors would receive the finest pediatric care, and soon be restored to vigorous health.

"I wish it were that simple," Grant replied. "A case of measles or mumps? No, sir. Far worse. The youngsters are innocent victims of a despicable crime."

"Certainly not in Philadelphia," I protested.

"Afraid so." The president's face was grim. "They've been kidnapped."

Vesper caught her breath. All of us, indeed, were too shocked to speak. Grant was the first to break the silence.

"Kidnapped, the boy and girl both. His Majesty put himself in touch with me immediately. Ordinary circumstances, I'd have set every last resource to work at getting them back. These aren't ordinary circumstances, and the emperor isn't an ordinary person."

"Then," said Vesper, "what are you going to do?"

"The lives of the youngsters have to be our first concern," said Grant. "No question. We don't dare risk their safety. As I figure it, there's only one thing to be done. We do as the kidnappers tell us."

"Give in?" returned Vesper. The dear girl's temperament is not one to let villainy hold sway unimpeded. "That's it? There has to be a better way."

"None practical," said Grant. "Dom Pedro agrees. There's a ransom, of course. A big one. Bigger than you could imagine. No matter. The emperor will pay it.

"So much for that part," Grant went on. "But there's another angle to this affair. It has to be kept absolutely secret. If word of it ever got out— There's a lot of very powerful, influential people who'd seize on this as one more example of the government's incompetence. The administration can't even protect two little children, let alone run the country. That's what they'd say, and they'd have it in every newspaper from here to the Territories."

"But it's not your fault," said Vesper.

"Doesn't signify," Grant replied. "It's just the kind of pretext they've been itching for. To stir up more trouble. I told you we were sitting on a powder keg. A thing like this could set it off. You'd see the nation torn apart. Same thing would happen in Brazil. Dom Pedro has his enemies, too. They'd jump at the chance to ruin him."

"I understand why it has to be a secret," said Vesper. "We'd all be glad to help, but what can we do that's any use? If the emperor's willing to pay and the kidnappers keep their part of the bargain—and why shouldn't they?—then it's settled."

"I suppose you could say that," replied Grant. "Yes, it's settled. Except for one final detail. Delivering the ransom. I'm here to ask: Will you do it?"

Before the president could say more, or Vesper could reply, I felt obliged to speak frankly.

"Our hearts go out to those unhappy infants and to His Majesty. Simple as it seems, however, this errand could involve considerable risk. Sir, with all respect, I cannot understand why you make such a request of Miss Holly. Is this not a task for someone in the emperor's own entourage? Or the Pinkerton detective service? Indeed, sir, I suggest our Philadelphia police, the nation's finest."

"No. None of them," said Grant. "Dom Pedro has received a letter of instructions. The terms are set down precisely. The ransom must be delivered in person, by none other than Miss Vesper Holly."

"But—but that is outrageous!" I cried. "Her presence demanded by some vile abductor? Some unknown, nameless criminal?"

"Not nameless," Grant said. "The letter is signed: *Dr. Desmond Helvitius.*"

❧ 3 ❧

The president's mere utterance of that vile monster's name was enough to make my gentle, sensitive Mary gasp and clap a hand over her mouth. Smiler and Slider, usually dauntless, exchanged uneasy glances. My blood, I confess, ran suddenly cold.

Vesper sat calmly and quietly, a thoughtful expression on her face. Her brilliant mind, I knew, was instantly analyzing all the implications of President Grant's announcement. At last, she turned to me.

"That's clever of him, Brinnie. Very neat."

"Abominable!" I exclaimed. "Helvitius on our native shores! In Philadelphia itself! Dear girl, he has struck at two innocent babes, the emperor of Brazil, our country, our city, and ourselves in a single blow!"

"That's what I mean," Vesper said. "Neat and economical. I wonder how he managed it. And why."

The president had been listening closely to our exchange. "I take it you know this Dr. Helvitius."

"We've met," said Vesper, "from time to time."

"Miss Holly understates the matter," I put in. "We are all too familiar with him. Sir, this archvillain has attempted to destroy us by dynamite bombs, by living burial, by exposure to the cruelest mental torture. He has even sought to exterminate us by means of an exploding sausage. That, sir, has been the nature of our relationship with Dr. Helvitius."

Though Grant had been immersed in politics for the past eight years, he was shocked by such ruthlessness.

"I understand," he said, after taking a few moments to compose himself, "why he named Miss Holly to deliver the ransom. The man's a rattlesnake I've never come up against a sidewinder like him, not even in Congress."

"This wretch," I declared, since Vesper herself did not reply, "this self-styled academic, this heartless murderer who boasts of his sensitivity to art and music has not only set a death trap, he brazenly dares Miss Holly to enter it."

"Brinnie," Vesper said to me, "I think President Grant recognizes clever strategy when he sees it."

"Yes," Grant said, "and I also recognize why you must refuse to deal with that reptile."

"I haven't said—" Vesper began.

"Miss Holly," said Grant, "I've already sent too many people out to die. No more. I won't ask a service from you that might cost your life."

"What will you do?" asked Vesper.

"I don't know." Grant shook his head. "Thank you for your time. I'll take up no more of it."

Grant would have risen, but a whoop from the hallway set him back into his chair.

"Beans! A hundred jars of beans for the palace at Knossos!"

I groaned and held my head.

It was The Weed.

I had forgotten he was in the house. The president's account of Helvitius's new villainy had driven all thoughts of The Weed from my mind. My heart sank as he came loping into the room.

Tobias Wistar Passavant—Vesper had nicknamed him "The Weed"—had arrived several months ago, unannounced and uninvited. He had returned from some sort of archeological expedition on the island of Crete. His previous occupations were vague, though he seemed to have had a great many; presently, he was attempting to decipher a number of inscriptions written in a completely unknown and baffling language. Aware of Dr. Holly's own research, he begged Vesper to allow him the use of her father's library. Vesper generously gave permission. This lanky, gawky individual had been in residence ever since. I guessed him to be about twenty-four, and to me it felt as if he had spent most of those years interrupting whatever I happened to be doing. Why Vesper and Mary put up with him went beyond human comprehension.

"Beans! Or maybe lentils. If I'm right, it's the key to the whole thing!"

The Weed was grinning all over his face. Excessively, like everything connected with him. His feet were too large, his legs too long, his ears—what could be seen of them under his untrimmed hair—were too big. He gave the impression of being everywhere at once. In brief, he was a one-man crowd.

"Tobias," I said sternly, "you intrude on a most serious and private matter. Do you not realize who is present?"

Until then, caught up by his jars of beans, he had not so much as glanced at anyone but Vesper.

"Who?" At last he turned his eyes on the president. "Oh. Why, hello there, Sam."

"Hello there, Toby." Grant smiled for the first time.

"Miss Holly," the president said, while I sat dumbstruck, "I had no idea this young fellow was a friend of yours."

"Or yours," replied Vesper.

The Weed—without being asked—flung himself into a chair. He leaned forward, elbows on his knees, hands clasped under his chin, which made him look something like a praying mantis, and assumed himself to be part of the conversation.

"Carrots," he said to Vesper—he had bestowed this name on her in exchange for the one she had given him. Unseemly, even disrespectful though it was, Vesper tolerated it. "What are you and Sam up to?"

"Mr. President," I whispered, once I had mastered my surprise and regained my voice, "the question of secrecy—"

"It's all right," Grant assured me. "The same way Miss Holly trusts you, I trust young Toby here. He has a head on his shoulders."

I said no more and refrained from speculating on what kind of muddle that head contained, beyond being filled with beans and lentils. This was not the moment to express my personal opinions.

In any case, with a clarity unexpected in a military man, Grant quickly reviewed the situation which had brought him here.

"*A fronte praecipitium a tergo lupi,* wouldn't you say?" remarked The Weed when Grant had finished. "A precipice in front of you, a wolf behind you."

"Tobias, please," I put in, "we all understand the problem."

"Sorry, sir. You're quite right." He turned to Vesper. "I don't know how to go at it. There's no good answer."

"Maybe not a good answer," said Vesper, "but only one. I've already decided. I'm going to do it."

Knowing Vesper as I did, her announcement came as no surprise. It was not her nature to turn from a challenge, least of all when the lives of innocent babes were at stake. I could not have been more proud of her. I could not have been more apprehensive.

"Dear girl," I said, "you must exercise utmost caution. You are putting yourself in that villain's clutches and at his mercy."

"Not if I can help it." Vesper now addressed Grant. "Mr. President—Sam—I'll do it if I have a free hand to make my own plans. I'll need help. From Brinnie and the twins. And Toby. If they'll agree to give it."

How could we refuse after the example of Philadelphia courage and duty she had set for us? Mary, too, offered her assistance, though naturally there could be no question of this gentle angel involving herself in any possible danger.

"I'm grateful to you." President Grant's aversion to shaking hands was well known—no doubt because he had

18

done so much of it—but he rose and stepped over to Vesper. Not only did he take her hand but kissed it with the gallantry befitting an officer, a gentleman, and our highest official. "I wouldn't have blamed you if you'd refused, but I'm glad you chose as you did."

It would be necessary, Grant went on, for us to go immediately to the emperor at his hotel, and he offered to put his carriage at our disposal. Vesper politely declined, preferring her own vehicle.

"Then, young lady, I'll go back to Washington City before they think I got lost," said Grant, "though some people might take that as cause for a celebration. You stay in touch with me. Telegraph if you need anything; I'll see that you get it."

The president halted at the door. "By the way, what do you know about—what's it called?—'Aronimink?'"

"It's an Indian word," answered The Weed, who had not been asked. "Lenni-Lenape for *beaver lodge.*"

"I'm not interested in beaver lodges," said Grant. "I mean: Where is it?"

When Vesper explained that this rustic locality lay a number of miles southeast of Strafford, Grant shook his head. "Too far to make a side trip. An old comrade-in-arms has a farm there. General Gallaway."

"Dapper Dan Gallaway?" Vesper was as familiar as we all were with the name of that colorful hero of our war between the states.

"None other." Grant half smiled in almost wistful recollection. "Had as much flash and fire as George Custer, and just as young. Not that any of us is young now. He's on the inactive list, writing his memoirs or some such nonsense." Grant sighed. "Good old Dapper Dan. We've had our differences and fallings-out. But he was always a good soldier. I had a notion I might look him up for old times' sake. Mend a few fences, too. I like to be on good terms with my officers. Never know when you need them. Well, some other day."

The president then took grateful leave of us. As soon as his carriage pulled away, Vesper asked the twins to hitch up Hengist and Horsa, her pair of dappled grays.

"I shall accompany you," declared Mary. "The poor empress will surely need the consolation of an older woman."

Vesper gladly agreed, and I could hardly object to such a mission of mercy. After putting down an ample supply of food for Moggie in case our return might be delayed, Vesper judged it wise for us to pack a few personal items.

"It's going to be too late for us to get home again tonight," she said. "We can sleep over in Philadelphia."

As we hurried to follow this practical suggestion, Vesper beckoned to Toby.

"You really are a weed. A rank one." She grinned at him. "Why didn't you tell me you knew Sam Grant?"

The Weed blushed bright crimson, another thing he did too much. "You never asked me."

4

Although Vesper pressed him for details, Toby shrugged off his acquaintance with the president. Instead, once we had settled into the carriage, he rattled away about ancient Cretan beans.

"It's the first clue to an unknown language. But whose? Early Greeks'? Minoans'? An undiscovered civilization's?"

I could have wished for a little less bounce in his enthusiasm. The carriage was roomy—Vesper had designed it, and the twins, with Yankee ingenuity, had built it to her specifications—but The Weed, flinging himself beside me, somehow managed to occupy most of the space. As to be expected. In the house, I could not enter a room without bumping into him on his way out. He was at the library desk when I wished to use it, or going up the stairs when I was coming down and coming down when I was going up. The mansion, years ago, had served as a station on the Underground Railroad, a haven for escaping slaves.

For this honorable purpose, a number of hidden passages and chambers had been added to the original construction. Had I ventured into the remotest part of that concealed maze, I am sure I would have stumbled over The Weed.

He and Vesper chatted away about Minoans and early Greeks as if they had nothing more serious on their minds. Thanks to the sustaining presence of Mary, the driving skills of Smiler and Slider, and the speed of Hengist and Horsa, the ride did not seem uncomfortably long to me. We reached Philadelphia by early evening and drew up at the intersection of our renowned Broad and Chestnut Streets.

If the reason for our excursion had been happier, I would have enjoyed the sight of our splendid metropolis. Gaslights glowed at almost every corner. Even at this hour, fashionably attired passersby strolled along the sidewalks. Hansom cabs and elegant private carriages crowded the thoroughfares. Our magnificent network of street railways, their well-ventilated cars drawn by spirited, though somewhat elderly, cart horses served the less affluent public. La Pierre House towered majestically a full four stories into the sky.

Smiler and Slider deposited us in front of the hotel and drove off to find a livery stable. We entered the spacious lobby, abundantly equipped with gleaming cuspidors and set about with luxuriant potted palms. The Weed strode ahead of us, straight to the registration desk, and demanded to see the manager immediately.

"Hello there, Toby," said the manager, who instantly appeared. "How have you been?"

"Look, Fred," The Weed replied, "we want to see

Dom Pedro—or whatever he's calling himself. Tell him Sam Grant sent us."

Never questioning his orders, the manager hurried to carry them out. Moments later, a gentleman-in-waiting came to conduct us to the mezzanine floor, entirely taken over by Dom Pedro and his entourage. We were immediately ushered into the largest suite and into the presence of the emperor himself.

Misfortune makes equals of us all. As Vesper presented us to His Majesty, Dom Pedro dispensed with formalities and gratefully took her hand.

"Miss Holly, I cannot sufficiently thank you." Dom Pedro responded in flawless English, though Vesper had spoken to him in his native Portuguese. Empress Theresa, silver haired and pleasantly matronly, greeted us with the same lack of ceremony. In fact, with spontaneous compassion, Mary held out her arms, and the two women embraced as if they were sisters in despair.

"We know some of what's happened," Vesper began. "I know what he wants as far as I'm concerned; I need to find out what Helvitius wants from you."

"I admire you all the more for putting yourself at such risk." Dom Pedro gravely inclined his head after Vesper explained why Helvitius had chosen her. If President Grant had seemed burdened by his office, Dom Pedro bore his rank with long-accustomed ease, having ruled his vast empire since the tender age of fifteen. Though strands of white threaded his beard, his handsome features had kept a youthful eagerness. Despite his imperial rank, all in all he seemed a reasonable sort of fellow, with a lively intelligence not often observed in monarchs. Indeed, during his reign of some thirty-five years, he had grown to be a most progressive, humane, and democratically minded ruler. Except for the accident of noble birth, he could have been a Philadelphian.

"First," the emperor went on, "I can tell you what I myself know." That morning, he related, little Januaria and her brother, Paulo, along with their governess, had emerged from admiring the Liberty Bell. A carriage drew up and they were forced to enter it. Driven then to La Pierre House, the governess was roughly ejected. The carriage and the children drove off instantly. The governess had been given a letter, which His Majesty now handed to Vesper.

"Sir," I said, while Vesper scanned the closely written page, "I understand that the ransom is large. Miss Holly has agreed to deliver it, but how shall it be transported? The despicable villain has no doubt demanded his price in gold. The weight would be considerable."

"On the contrary, Professor Garrett," replied the emperor. "It can be carried in the slenderest packet."

"That's right, Brinnie." Vesper glanced up. "Helvitius doesn't want a sackful of money."

"Alas, not," said the emperor. "He demands far more: licenses, formal agreements, contracts. Nothing less than the sole rights to exploit my country's resources. Gold, rubber, coffee, all our natural wealth, in effect, will come under his control. He offers to pay my government a share of his profits. It will be a pittance compared with his own enormous gains."

"What it comes down to," said Vesper, "is Helvitius practically owning Brazil."

24

"I fear so," said the emperor. "The result would be untold riches for him; for my people, wretched poverty."

"Is there no limit to the scoundrel's greed?" I burst out. "It is matched only by his arrogance! How does he dare make such a demand?"

"Easy," said Vesper. "He has the children to bargain with." Her face turned grave. "Brinnie, he's serious about this. They could die if the emperor doesn't meet his terms."

Empress Theresa, leaning on Mary's arm, now spoke anxiously to Vesper. "Senhorita, the children were entrusted to us. We must regain them, no matter what the cost."

"That's why I'm here," Vesper assured her. "It just sticks in my craw, letting Helvitius pocket a fortune and wreck your country."

"My only concern is for the children and your own safety," said the emperor. "The ransom is of no importance."

"We can't weigh lives against money," replied Vesper. "No question of that. But—not important? You yourself said it would mean poverty—"

"It would," said the emperor, "if I intended to pay this ransom. Which I do not."

5

"But—Your Majesty, Sam Grant told me it was settled, you were willing to pay. I understood I was delivering the ransom."

"Please"—the emperor smiled a little—"since you refer to your president as 'Sam,' I offer you a similar token of friendship. I would take it as a compliment from a most valiant young woman if you were to call me simply 'Dom Pedro.'

"I have prepared all the necessary documents," he went on, as Vesper acknowledged his imperial courtesy, "written in my own hand exactly according to my instructions. Yes, you shall deliver them."

Vesper looked questioningly at Dom Pedro, who drew a sheaf of papers from his breast pocket and handed them to her.

"I believe I am a man of honor," Dom Pedro said. "My word is my bond. In this case, Dr. Helvitius is entitled neither to my honor nor to my word. These licenses are worthless."

"They look fine to me." The Weed had been reading over Vesper's shoulder. "At first glance, anyway."

"Tobias," I muttered, "if you would refrain—"

"They are entirely legal." Dom Pedro's fine brow darkened angrily. "However, I have been forced to sign them—under duress, I believe is your phrase. When I return to Brazil and Helvitius attempts to enforce them, I shall declare them null and void.

"I shall renounce them," Dom Pedro declared. "It is my imperial right to do so, given just cause. Can any cause be more just? Yes, I shall break my word—a word extorted by this vile criminal—and do it with a clear conscience. For all practical purposes, these licenses will be useless scraps of paper."

"As the scoundrel deserves!" I cried. "No! What he deserves is the severest punishment. I pray that somehow it will be meted out to him."

Vesper did not seem as pleased as I was at seeing the monster's plan so properly thwarted. "I'd been wondering if you could repeal the licenses after you'd written them. Yes, that's good. It's only half of it, though. The other half is making him give back the children."

She returned to scrutinizing the letter. "He claims he'll hand them over after I deliver the licenses. He's set our meeting for tomorrow midnight The Pepper Pot."

"Soup?" I inquired, perplexed by what Philadelphia's world-renowned potage had to do with kidnapping.

"Sir," The Weed helpfully put in, "that must be the Pepper Pot Tavern, past Front Street. By the river, close to the docks. A rough sort of place, you know."

I did not know. Nor did I wish to ask how he had gained familiarity with a low dive, perhaps a den of thieves. A few such establishments, regrettably, marred our city.

"I'm to go there," Vesper said. "A private room's been reserved in my name. I'm to ask the tavern keeper."

"The villain's plan is clear!" I exclaimed. "He has hired a murderous ruffian, or a band of them, to set upon you. Paid assassins! They will take your life and ransom both. I insist on accompanying you, but I cannot allow you to enter an obvious trap."

"Last place in the world I intend to be is a stranger's back room," Vesper said. "There must be a way around that. Even so, his plan isn't clear at all. Do me in then and there? It could bring the police into it, and more public notice than Helvitius likes. It's not his style. Besides, I doubt that he enjoys having two scared children on his hands."

"You cannot mean that he will keep his part of the bargain?"

"No, I don't expect him to," Vesper said. "And yet—Brinnie, I don't know what to make of this. It's tricky no matter how you you look at it. Some other things bother me, too."

Turning her attention from the ransom note, Vesper asked if she might speak with the governess, Senhora Da Costa. Dom Pedro sent for her, and she arrived moments later from an adjoining apartment. I expected her to be distraught. On the contrary. Her face was pale not with grief but anger, at herself as much as at Helvitius.

"The children were abducted through my fault alone." Senhora Da Costa stood stiffly drawn up to her full height,

28

as tall as Vesper. On her finely chiseled, even aristocratic countenance, was an expression of steely resolve. "Their welfare was my responsibility. I failed in it."

"Senhora Da Costa," the empress murmured, "you cannot entirely blame yourself."

"I can and do," the governess replied. "Whatever steps are taken to recover Januaria and Paulo, I ask for some part in helping Senhorita Holly. If risks are to be run, let me be the one to do so."

"We'll see about that later," Vesper said, after thanking the governess for her courageous offer. "Right now, I'd like you to tell me every detail you remember. There might be some sort of clue."

The governess could reveal little more than what Dom Pedro had already recounted. She did add that three men had been present; they had threatened her with revolvers; they had spoken English, though she could not be certain whether they were American or of some other nationality. She did not recall in which direction the carriage drove away.

Vesper thanked Senhora Da Costa, promising to ask her further assistance if needed. By this time, Smiler and Slider had arrived. Vesper presented them to Dom Pedro, who shook each warmly by the hand. An enthusiastic amateur scientist, the emperor took a keen interest in all natural phenomena and started to question the twins about their close fraternal bond.

Vesper pointed out that it was growing late. She proposed renting rooms for all of us elsewhere in the hotel. Dom Pedro insisted, however, on lodging us in some of his own apartments, and we were quickly installed in a suite as luxurious as the fabled La Pierre House could provide.

Among ourselves now, Vesper felt free to express what she had been reluctant to say before Dom Pedro.

"Something tells me," she began, "this whole business isn't as straightforward as it looks."

To me, nothing could be more so. Helvitius had, quite simply, struck on the diabolical scheme of using two helpless youngsters as pawns to enrich himself and to seek revenge on Vesper. What, I asked, could be clearer?

"For one thing," replied Vesper, "Helvitius says he'll do away with the children if Dom Pedro doesn't pay up."

"Can you doubt for an instant that he will carry out his threat?" I said. "He would show them not the slightest mercy. He would extinguish their lives and enjoy a hearty breakfast afterward."

"Yes," Vesper said, "but if he does away with the children he has nothing to bargain with. Unless he gets his hands on those licenses first. Which leads to what bothers me the most.

"Helvitius is a scoundrel, not a fool. Doesn't he realize that Dom Pedro can nullify those agreements? Did he overlook that little detail? That might be the one flaw in his scheme. Or doesn't he care? If that's the case, why? The only one who can tell us is Helvitius himself.

"Another thing," added Vesper. "Which came first, the chicken or the egg? Did Helvitius start with the idea of getting back at us and stumble on a neat way to do it? Or were we an afterthought? I'm only curious. It makes no difference in how we deal with him."

"In any case," I asked, "how do we deal with him?"

"I don't know yet," admitted Vesper. "At least, we

have plenty of time to think about it. Until tomorrow midnight, that is."

Vesper, during this, had been pacing the room. Her powerful intellect, grappling with these questions, had turned her restless. The Weed, sitting quietly in an armchair, reached into his pocket and fished out a length of string, which he knotted into a loop and slipped over his hands.

"Tobias, for goodness sake," I said to him, "what are you doing?"

"Cat's cradle, sir. The Samoans are amazing at it. You should see the patterns they come up with."

"I am quite aware of what it is," I replied. "I merely wish to know why, of all times, you choose to indulge in it."

"Helps me think, sir." The Weed was always infuriatingly respectful. "Try it?"

"I will," said Vesper, as I declined the invitation. She left off pacing and sat on a hassock across from The Weed. She learned quickly, of course, and the pair of them silently exchanged the evermore complex net, absorbed in the childish diversion.

Despite President Grant's recommendation of him, I had reservations concerning The Weed. The Passavants had been an old, respected Philadelphia family, prominent in the arts and sciences. Tobias, last of the line, had obviously inherited none of his forebears' capacities. An individual who fritters away his time deciphering obscure inscriptions, is on familiar terms with members of the hotel-keeping trade, and diverts himself with a piece of string—none of these traits reassured me.

Vesper had not troubled to change her costume. She

31

still wore her red caftan. A recollection struck me with sudden, terrible force. She had worn it the day Mary and I first met her. The unreasonable but chilling thought came unbidden to my mind: that I was seeing her as I had seen her for the first time and, now, for the last.

I shuddered and tried to dismiss the irrational notion. Several moments passed before I became conscious of Mary's hand on my shoulder.

"Come along, dear Brinnie. You need your sleep."

Vesper and The Weed were still playing cat's cradle when I followed Mary into our apartments. Surprisingly, I slept soundly. I wished I had not, for I was plagued by dreams of huge webs forming and reforming in constantly shifting patterns and, at their center, a lurking spider.

CHAPTER

6

Whether The Weed's cat's cradle stimulated Vesper's thoughts I very much doubted. Her mental powers hardly needed a loop of string to inspire them. In any case, when we met for breakfast next morning, Vesper announced that she had a plan, at least the beginnings of one.

"That's more than I had last night," she said. "So, it's a start."

The Weed had not yet appeared. When we went to fetch him from his room, we found him standing on one long leg, the other bent so that the sole of his right foot rested beside his left knee. His eyes were shut, his hands clasped under his chin, and on his face was a blissful smile.

"It's something he does," Vesper said, as if that were explanation enough. "His meditating posture. The Gonds do it in India."

I pointed out that he was not a Gond and we were in Philadelphia.

"I've been meaning to try it," said Vesper. "He says it does him good."

I fervently hoped so.

Meantime, The Weed had opened one eye, then the other, and wished us a good morning. It took him a while to unfold himself. By the time the three of us returned to the salon, Smiler and Slider were halfway through breakfast. My eggs had gone cold.

"So far," Vesper began after Mary had poured The Weed his third cup of tea, "Helvitius is the one giving us orders, telling us what we have to do. He's pulling our strings as if we were marionettes. I'd like to change that around. I want to pull his strings for a change.

"Now, what I've tried to figure out first is this meeting at the Pepper Pot. Brinnie says it's a trap. I'm sure he's right. Only I don't know what kind of trap. I want to be there—but not be there. If it turns out I'll need those licenses, I want to have them with me—but not have them, so they can't be forced out of me.

"That part's easy enough"—Vesper glanced at The Weed—"you'll be the one actually carrying the papers. For the rest, you and the twins go down to the waterfront. Take a quiet look at the Pepper Pot. Then buy seaman's clothes for all of us."

Vesper broke off at the arrival of Dom Pedro and Senhora Da Costa. Dom Pedro apologized for the absence of Empress Theresa, too overwrought to join us.

"If things go the way I hope," said Vesper, "she'll soon feel a lot better."

Vesper then asked Dom Pedro if one of his retainers could drive our carriage that night. The emperor was glad to oblige, and Senhora Da Costa offered her own services. She considered it her responsibility to go with us. Vesper, at first, was reluctant to add another member to our group. The governess insisted so firmly, however, that Vesper finally nodded.

"All right," she said. "You'll stay in the carriage, though. If there's trouble, you'll go back to the hotel and warn the emperor.

"Aunt Mary," she went on, "you'll be our anchor. Stay here with Dom Pedro and the empress. In case of emergency, you'll know best what to do. Brinnie and I will be at the Pepper Pot."

"Dear girl," I reminded her, "you said you did not wish to be there."

"We won't be," said Vesper. "Not in a back room, anyway."

As the twins and The Weed set off on their errands, Vesper turned to Dom Pedro. "Something I wanted to ask. Do the children's parents know what's happened?"

"I have not yet sent word to them," replied Dom Pedro. "I shall do so, of course. Nor have I telegraphed my daughter. Princess Isabella is regent in my absence, she has full authority to act on my behalf and do whatever is necessary. She, too, must be made aware of this unfortunate event."

"Hold off a while," Vesper advised. "They can't help us, there's no use upsetting them. What I'm hoping," she added, "is when you do send word, you can tell them the children are safe again and it's all happily over."

"So I pray," replied Dom Pedro. "President Grant has surely told you of the need for secrecy. He has his enemies and, alas, I have my own. The high aristocracy has never ceased to oppose my democratic reforms. They would like nothing better than to claim I was unfit to rule. The emperor junketing abroad and losing, perhaps, the lives of two children? The outcry would lead to my dethronement and the end of my hopes for Brazil. No, nothing of this dreadful affair must go beyond those immediately concerned. I have every confidence in my daughter's discretion. I cannot say likewise for her husband. He is not in sympathy with my programs. As for his judgment and common sense, what little he has—"

Dom Pedro waved away that subject and smiled ruefully at me. "I should not let family problems intrude. However, speaking not as an emperor but as a loving father, I must say it bewilders me how an intelligent young woman such as Isabella could develop an unaccountable affection for a most unlikely individual."

Sorry though I was for Dom Pedro, I was delighted that Vesper would certainly never do likewise.

The most boring aspect of any hazardous enterprise is waiting to do it. The hours before our assigned meeting at the Pepper Pot dragged by endlessly. The only break in the nerve-racking monotony came that afternoon, when The Weed and the twins returned, bringing the clothing Vesper had requested.

"They're very good secondhand," Smiler assured me. "As secondhand as any I've seen."

"Mr. Toby knew a first rate pawnbroker on Front Street," added Slider. "He accommodated us as nice as you'd want."

My bundle of canvas trousers and blue jacket wafted an aroma suggesting they had been worn, at one time or another, by our entire merchant navy. Vesper's similar costume included a Greek fisherman's cap which would allow her to tuck up her hair inside it. The Weed and the twins had acquired stained shirts and bespattered pairs of slops. They were all quite satisfied with their purchases.

We had nothing to do but wait. Enforced idleness increased my apprehension. Vesper had told me the general outline of her plan. I did not much like it, but could offer no better suggestion. And so we waited. I tried to maintain at least the appearance of tranquility, without great success. The Weed was as cheerful as if he were going to a party.

Vesper, for her part, passed the time chatting with the emperor. Dom Pedro, she learned, had his own laboratory where he conducted experiments in chemistry and physics, and had even tried to develop a new type of electrical generator.

"I am eager to see the new machinery displayed at the Exposition," he told Vesper. "The Corliss engine in particular. It is, I understand, a most advanced example of industrial design."

He went on to tell us that he and President Grant would officially open the Exposition by starting this immense machine. "We shall both turn the master valve and, by our simple gesture, the Corliss engine will spring to life and provide power to all other equipment in Machinery Hall. A splendid moment, the dawn of a happy new era."

Dom Pedro's enthusiasm faded. "But I shall have no heart to attend the ceremonies, unless the children are safe by then. Yet, I must do so. My country would be dishonored if its emperor were absent."

"Staying away can't help," said Vesper. "You must go, no matter what. I'm counting on having Paulo and Januaria back long before then."

Her confidence reassured the emperor, who went on to describe a new device a friend of his intended to exhibit. The young fellow had put together some kind of box which, he claimed, could send the human voice through a length of wire. The inventor's name eluded me, I had no interest in such a harebrained notion. Vesper, of course, was fascinated.

After a light supper—The Weed attacked his plate with an exuberant appetite matched only by Vesper's—we put on our nautical costumes. The Weed stowed the packet of papers under his jacket, then he and the twins departed on foot. Following Vesper's instructions, they had already scouted out vantage points around the tavern and would post themselves there.

With Mary's blessings and the emperor's anxious wishes for a safe outcome, Vesper and I climbed into our carriage, awaiting us in front of La Pierre House. Senhora Da Costa sat in brooding silence across from us. A little distance from the waterfront, Vesper ordered the driver to halt. He and the governess would remain there until we returned.

We made the rest of our way on foot, attracting no attention from the passersby and corner loungers, all dressed as roughly as ourselves. The waterfront of any great metropolis is rarely a quarter of fashionable elegance. Despite the vista of our majestic Delaware River and the tall masts of vessels moored at the piers, our thriving port gave off something of a raffish air; the result, no doubt, of the influence of so many foreign sailors of dubious moral standards. In front of a busy tattoo parlor, a few longshoremen consumed a local delicacy: enormous soft pretzels daubed with mustard. Elsewhere, seafarers staggered from various places of refreshment. A couple of dockers had chosen to settle some disagreement by fisticuffs and ear-biting.

I calmed any uneasiness I felt by reminding myself that Philadelphia was, nevertheless, the City of Brotherly Love.

We found the Pepper Pot easily enough. With its scabby plaster walls and tightly shuttered windows, it conveyed no atmosphere of cheerful welcome. Vesper, even so, stepped boldly into the common eating room as if she had been there a dozen times before. She chose a table affording us a clear view of the door. The few other patrons occupying the dimly lit room hardly glanced at us. No sooner had we seated ourselves on a couple of rickety chairs than the waiter, presumably according to the custom of the house, immediately and without being asked, brought us steaming bowls of the substance which gave the tavern its name. Unlike Vesper, I had no appetite for my portion.

It was well before the appointed hour, as Vesper had planned. Waiting, she rehearsed our intentions.

"We just sit here, Brinnie, and keep an eye on the door. I'm counting on somebody coming in to look for us. I don't expect it will be Helvitius himself, but whoever heads for the back room won't find us there. We'll see what they do next. If they leave, we'll go after them. Weed and the twins are watching, too, and they'll follow us. Maybe we can find out where Helvitius is and where he's keeping the children.

"If he's really going to stick to his bargain, we'll have the papers ready. If he isn't, I'm sure he won't harm the children unless he has the licenses. Or me. Or both. No matter what, we'll have thrown him off balance. He'll wonder what's happened, and that should pretty well puzzle him. He'll have to get in touch with us again. When he does, I'll be the one calling the tune.

"I'll tell him we'll trade the licenses for Januaria and Paulo. Not in some back room, though. Right out in the open. The middle of Rittenhouse Square, maybe the lobby of La Pierre House. See what he says to that."

She hesitated. "Dear Brinnie—have I done right? We can't just play by his rules. It's a risk whatever we do. All the more if I've gone at it the wrong way."

A new arrival had entered. Not Helvitius or some ruffianly henchman, but Senhora Da Costa.

Catching sight of us, the governess hurried over and sat facing us. She bent forward and rapidly whispered.

"Senhorita Holly," she began before Vesper could ask why she had not stayed in the carriage, "the driver has gone back to the hotel."

"Why?" demanded Vesper. "What's happened?"

"He will inform the emperor that you have been unavoidably delayed, and that Senhora Garrett must return to her home without you."

"My dear madam," I broke in, with much irritation, "how have you had the presumption? You took such a

40

step on your own authority? You may well have spoiled our careful preparations."

"Your plans have changed," replied the governess. "Be so good as to come with me immediately."

"Madam," I protested, "for what reason?"

"A good one," muttered Vesper. "She's pointing a gun at you."

❧ 7 ❧

Senhora Da Costa had indeed drawn a revolver from her purse. Even Vesper's genius in foreseeing unexpected turns of events could not have extended to treachery on the part of a trusted retainer, especially one whose noble duty was the nurture of the young. If the dear girl was taken aback, it was by astonishment, not fear. Vesper has faced a variety of lethal weapons without losing her natural poise and dignity. She continued eating her soup.

"Go with you? What if we don't?" After a moment, Vesper put down her spoon and looked squarely at the governess. "Somehow I doubt that you'll really shoot me. Here? Now? I don't think so."

I did. In an establishment like the Pepper Pot, the occasional fatal assault would attract little notice, if any.

"No, I will not shoot you," replied Senhora Da Costa. "Only Professor Garrett."

Senhora Da Costa's icy tone alarmed me as much as the weapon she held.

"Traitress!" I cried. "To betray your emperor is despicable in itself. But—this? Madam, your behavior is monstrous!"

"I am sure it is," replied Senhora Da Costa. "Nevertheless, you will do as I say."

Vesper seemed ready to obey, for my sake if not her own. I could not allow it. Senhora Da Costa had forfeited the courtesy to which her womanhood entitled her. I sprang to my feet and seized the only available means of defense: my steaming bowl of pepper pot.

Without remorse or hesitation, I flung the vessel and its peppery contents at Senhora Da Costa's head. Or so I would have done. That instant, the bowl was struck out of my hand, and a pair of beefy arms held me fast. Vesper had risen from her chair to come to my aid. She, too, was gripped by another patron.

"Sir, you misunderstand," I cried. "We are the innocent victims, not the aggressors. That woman"—I tried to point an accusing finger at the governess—"has threatened our lives. See, she is armed."

The ruffian ignored my explanation. Senhora Da Costa gave me a hard smile. "Resistance is futile. Dr. Helvitius foresaw some trickery by Senhorita Holly and made arrangements accordingly. The entire tavern has been hired for the occasion. All these men are in his employ."

Only then did I notice that the tavern keeper had posted himself by the front door. If any legitimate customers had been admitted by error, they chose to disregard our plight. The others looked on coldly, as they had been paid to do. To think that Philadelphians were open to this wholesale bribery pained me even more than Senhora Da Costa's treachery.

"Brinnie," suggested Vesper, "we'd better go with her."

Another couple of ruffians had stepped over to join their fellows. With a burly docker on each side of us gripping our arms, we were hauled through the eating room and out a small back door. Senhora Da Costa followed closely. She had covered the revolver with her purse but still kept the weapon trained on us.

"Go quietly," she warned. "If I must, I will shoot both of you."

I did not doubt her sincerity. Vesper, nevertheless, did what she could to impede our forced progress. As they hustled us down a twisting alleyway to Front Street and from there toward the piers, she deliberately slipped on the wet cobbles, dragged her feet, and strained against our captors' grips.

Surely by now, as I murmured to Vesper, The Weed and the twins would have seen our predicament. We could still hope for rescue.

"Not likely," muttered Vesper. "They're watching the front, not the back. If they saw the governess, they'd only think she was bringing a message or something. No reason to suspect what she was up to."

The passersby and street idlers would have no cause for suspicion either. To them, we were merely a party of jostling, high-spirited shipmates and their female companion: an altogether ordinary sight.

A pretzel vendor trundled his pushcart across our path. He wheeled his vehicle toward us, urging us to sample his wares. One of our captors gruffly ordered him away. The obstinate vendor continued to approach, blocking our way.

With a curse, our abductor shoved the cart aside. The hapless purveyor of pretzels tripped and stumbled into our midst.

"Weed!" Vesper shouted in happy recognition.

At first, I hardly believed my eyes. Yet, indeed, there he was with his oversized grin, his eyes eagerly alight, looking rather pleased with himself.

"Run for it," he advised, as he made to grapple the nearest ruffian.

We might have broken free had it not been for the pretzel cart. The Weed fought furiously—I had to give him that much credit—but, in his enthusiasm, he entangled himself with his vehicle, which overturned and sent him sprawling while pretzels flew in all directions; another instant and the ruffian was upon him.

Brandishing her pistol, Senhora Da Costa snapped out an order. Leaving their comrade to deal with The Weed, our abductors tightened their grip and sent us plunging headlong down the street, half wrestling, half dragging us with such brute force that Vesper's determined struggles, as well as my own, proved useless.

In a quick backward glance, I saw The Weed on his feet again. He had armed himself with one of the wooden rods on which his pretzels had been stacked and was belaboring his opponent about the head. I thought I also glimpsed Smiler and Slider.

By then a circle of onlookers had closed around The Weed. He vanished in their midst, and so, too, vanished our first and last hope of escape. Under the threatening revolver of the governess, manhandled by the dockers, we stumbled down to a landing. A trim little steam launch waited, its engine already churning, and we were compelled to board. Three crewmen took us into their keeping while Senhora Da Costa climbed after us.

Leaving our original abductors behind, the launch headed for the middle of the Delaware. Our fate had worsened, if that were possible, for the vessel's crew were even more villainous looking than our former captors.

Vesper has a fine sense of when to resist and when to yield. She settled herself as comfortably as she could in the narrow quarters amidships. "All right, what do you want from us?"

"From you, nothing," replied the governess, still pointing the revolver. "My part is done. What Dr. Helvitius may demand is not my concern."

"You're not much concerned about Januaria and Paulo, either," said Vesper.

"Clearly she is not," I put in. "Heartless wretch!"

"I have every concern for them," said Senhora Da Costa. "I am assured they will not come to harm. In the short time I have known them, I have grown fond of the little ones and they of me."

"Short time?" said Vesper. "I thought you'd always been their governess."

"Your impression is incorrect," replied Senhora Da Costa. "Their parents employed me a few days before the emperor and the children left Brazil. Their governess had fallen suddenly ill."

"Suddenly," said Vesper, "but not accidentally."

Senhora Da Costa nodded. "Dr. Helvitius arranged that event. He also provided me with the most excellent credentials and recommendations. The parents were overjoyed to engage a new governess who came so opportunely."

"A serpent in the bosom of a happy family!" I exclaimed. "Helvitius, I see, had no difficulty finding a faithless servant eager to do his bidding."

"Servant?" Senhora Da Costa's chin shot up, and her dark eyes flashed. "If you believe that of me, I have played my part well. My true name—which I shall not reveal to you—is borne proudly by one of the oldest families of Brazil. Dom Pedro would recognize it all too well, though he has never laid eyes on me until this journey."

"An aristocrat?" I was shocked. "Then your conduct is not only despicable but incomprehensible."

"I don't understand it either," admitted Vesper. "I can see what Helvitius is after, he's tried the same sort of thing before. What I can't see is why you'd have anything to do with him."

It became suddenly clear to me. The wretched woman was completely addled by her emotions. "Madam," I declared, "though it seems impossible for any human being to entertain tender feelings for that villain, I gather you have developed some inscrutable affection for the scoundrel."

"Affection?" Senhora Da Costa curled her lip. "I loathe and despise the creature. When he sought me out and offered me this opportunity, I accepted. For one reason only. Vengeance."

Senhora Da Costa voiced that last word with cold anger. "Our code of honor demands it. Revenge is my duty, my obligation not my pleasure."

"You can't want revenge on two children," said Vesper. "It must be their parents."

"No," Senhora Da Costa sharply replied. "Dom

47

Pedro. He alone is the object of my vengeance. For the sake of my late father and his memory."

"Odd sort of memorial, wouldn't you say?" Vesper murmured to me.

Senhora Da Costa ignored the comment and went on, "Not long ago, Dom Pedro publicly vowed to abolish slavery, to free all Indians and Africans in servitude throughout Brazil."

"Good idea," remarked Vesper. "It's about time. I say bravo for Dom Pedro."

Senhora Da Costa glared at her. "You do not realize the consequences. Emancipation strikes at the very roots of our family fortune: our plantations of rubber and coffee, our gold mines. Dom Pedro promised compensation. It would not have made up for my family's loss. Indeed, it threatened the way of life of all the great landowners.

"My father, along with others, opposed Dom Pedro. They tried to overthrow him—and failed. They were forced into exile and, worse, into disgrace."

"Sounds fair enough to me," said Vesper. "Dom Pedro could have had them shot, I suppose. They got off pretty easily. After all, they wanted to get rid of him. That's treason, isn't it?"

"Dom Pedro is the traitor," snapped Senhora Da Costa. "A traitor to his class. My father had no misgivings. He only regretted his failure. On his deathbed, he made me swear to avenge him. And so I shall."

Senhora Da Costa had grown quite exercised during her account. Her eyes smoldered, her hands so trembled with rage that I wished she would point the revolver in some other direction. Any Philadelphian would have com-

48

mended the actions of Dom Pedro, and Vesper obviously wished to say more along those lines. Senhora Da Costa, however, clamped her teeth shut and spoke no further of the subject. Just as well. A steam launch speeding down the Delaware with a vengeful Brazilian holding a gun did not provide a forum for reasonable discussion.

Vesper, too, remained silent. For my part, I had to reflect on the irony of fate that had turned us from rescuers into victims. Meantime, the launch chugged on rapidly over the waves of the mighty Delaware. Even in our present misfortune, I could not help but be moved by the sight of our noble waterway. Admittedly, it had none of the tropical flamboyance of the Amazon or the sweep of the Mississippi. It flowed majestically but with a certain Quaker modesty; it was a good, sensible river. Our enormous Philadelphia moon turned the tide to silver; the invigorating breeze wafted aromas of vegetation along the shore. Had our circumstances been different, I would have enjoyed the outing.

Vesper gently nudged me and made a quick motion with her head. Some distance astern, barely visible, another vessel followed in our wake. My heart leaped as I allowed myself to hope that somehow The Weed and the twins had come after us.

Unfortunately, Senhora Da Costa also noticed the vessel. She made no comment, only tightened her grip on the revolver and watched us like a hawk, not that it would have been possible, in any case, for Vesper to signal the other boat.

"Where's she taking us?" Vesper murmured after some time. "Out to sea?"

At first, I suspected that might be the case. I glimpsed the lights of the United States Naval Station off to starboard—how I wished our gallant sailors could know our plight—but the launch changed course, rounding that installation and heading into the gentle reaches of the Schuylkill River.

The vessel astern continued following. I prayed for it to overtake us. Yet the distance between the two crafts remained the same. I did not dare consult my watch, lest Senhora Da Costa misinterpret my reaching into my pocket, but I calculated it to be nearly dawn.

The launch bore us steadily upriver. Vesper stifled a cry of dismay. As we made for shore, the vessel which had so long kept us in sight now suddenly vanished and, with it, all our hopes.

"Disembark. Quickly," ordered Senhora Da Costa as the launch slid alongside a pier. "Dr. Helvitius will be eager to greet you."

"Can't say the same," replied Vesper, as we climbed from the launch. Senhora Da Costa and the crewmen prodded us along a wooden walkway. From what little I could glimpse, we had come ashore at some abandoned loading dock or industrial terminus. A little distance from the riverside rose the tin-roofed sheds and storage buildings of a freight station, a shattered water tower, a pile of rusted implements: all in all, in the first gray streaks of dawn, as bleak and dismal as my own spirits.

"At least, we'll find out what he's up to," said Vesper. "We'll know more than we did before."

More than we wanted to, in my opinion. Vesper, nevertheless, stepped out bravely and we continued past the freight yards. Moored at the last pier was the largest oceangoing yacht I ever saw. The long, sweeping hull was jet black, hardly visible in the dim light. The tall spires of the masts soared so high that their tops vanished in the mist. Vesper, always appreciative of excellence in nautical design, murmured admiration.

"Helvitius couldn't just go and buy that somewhere. He must have had it built. Handsome piece of work."

To me, it was more threatening than otherwise; the crew, even worse. Judging from the sailors on watch, as we climbed the gangway to the deck of polished teak-wood, Helvitius must have dredged the lowest waterfront dives of Hamburg, Marseille, and Boston to assemble such a company. Among them, in headcloths and kiltlike sarongs, stood a few of those infamous Malayan lascars, the most brutal of any in the nautical profession.

Grinning wickedly, eyes glittering in the lantern lights, a couple of lascars took us into custody. Senhora Da Costa put away the revolver. She had no need of it. In their waistbands, the lascars carried the dreadful Malayan creese, that wavy-bladed dagger as efficient and deadly in their hands as any firearm.

With Senhora Da Costa following, they conducted us into the main stateroom, as luxurious as our quarters in La Pierre House. Vesper glanced at the display of oil paintings, a large globe set in a carved wooden frame, the Persian carpets, and the mahogany captain's table.

"He doesn't stint himself," she remarked. "You can say that much for him."

We waited some long moments, the lascars watching our every move. At last, a door opened at the far end of the stateroom and in strolled the most abominable fiend it had ever been our misfortune to encounter. He looked in marvelous health and high spirits, comfortably attired in a silk dressing gown. His shock of white hair was elegantly barbered. His features were deeply tanned; the wretch, no doubt, had been sunning himself on the beaches of Rio de

52

Janeiro and Ipanema. Also, the disgusting fellow reeked of expensive cologne.

"Welcome aboard the *Minotaur*." Dr. Helvitius flashed a mouthful of powerful teeth. "It is more commodious than my previous vessel, would you not agree? And more suitable to my purposes."

"That depends on your purposes," Vesper said.

"You know them." Helvitius lowered his large, muscular frame into a leather chair behind the captain's table. "I made them clear in my letter of instructions which, as I expected, you did not obey."

"The ransom of innocent children!" I burst out. "Monster! Of all your vile deeds, this is the most despicable. For one who arrogantly pretends to scholarship and high culture, you, sir, have sunk to the lowest depths."

"My dear Professor Garrett," replied Helvitius, "allow me to disagree. I have risen, indeed, to new heights above all my former endeavors." He inclined his head toward Vesper. "Despite the efforts of Miss Holly to prevent me.

"However, it is profitless to discuss bygones. My mood is one of happy anticipation, especially with the approach of your marvelous Philadelphia Centennial Exposition, an event worthy of your great city. I certainly plan to attend. Alas, you will not be in a position to do likewise. I regret that. You would have found it in every way spectacular. But now"—his tone suddenly hardened—"of immediate importance: the documents. You have tried to deal falsely with me, Miss Holly. You have failed to do as I ordered. I shall overlook that. But I shall ask you once, and once only: Where are the licenses?"

"I don't have them," replied Vesper. "Did you really think I'd bring them with me?"

"I confess it is not always easy to foresee your actions." Helvitius leaned his bulk across the table and cast a baleful eye on Vesper. "I want those papers, and I shall get them one way or another. You say you do not have them? I do not wish to insult you by doubting your word. The question, however, is easily settled. You and Professor Garrett will submit to a thorough search. I regret the offense to your sensibilities. My lascars will be as courteous as possible."

"I'm sure." Vesper's glance did not waver even at this threat of unspeakable outrage. But such indignity was not to be tolerated. I shook my fist at the depraved monster.

"Sir, if you or your hirelings dare to lay so much as a finger on either of us—"

"She is telling the truth," Senhora Da Costa quickly put in. "I know for a fact that she does not have the papers. They are carried by a Senhor Passavant, one of her companions."

"That's right," said Vesper. "He has them, there's nothing you can do about it."

"I have reason to believe Senhor Passavant and the two others attempted to follow," added Senhora Da Costa. "I sighted a boat of some sort behind us, and I assume they had managed to obtain it."

"Excellent," said Helvitius. "I am confident that Miss Holly's companions will find her."

"They're gone," said Vesper. "I think they lost us."

"I think they did not," returned Helvitius. "We shall await their arrival."

"And then?" said Vesper.

"Why, we shall welcome them, Miss Holly. We shall welcome them with open arms."

"Suppose they don't come?" said Vesper.

Helvitius shrugged. "I shall be in an even stronger position to enforce my demands. Instead of merely two, I shall claim to have four hostages. Your friends must, ultimately, deliver the ransom."

"Hold on," said Vesper. "You said 'claim.' What do you mean by that?"

"I shall claim you are all alive and well. Whether that will be, in fact, the case—I have not yet decided. There are persuasive arguments for and against your continued existence."

"Does that apply to the children?" demanded Vesper. "Where are they? I want to see them. Right now."

"Quite impossible," said Helvitius. "They are not available. You and Professor Garrett would do better to be concerned for yourselves. As for your friends, my men are prepared to greet them. For your own sake, you should hope they will soon arrive. Otherwise, it will be far more difficult for you. However, we must fortify ourselves with patience. We shall wait."

And so we did, and it was as painful a time as I had ever spent. Smiling with anticipation, Helvitius leaned back in his chair. The lascars stood motionless, their eyes never leaving us. I had no inclination to make small talk with that arrogant scoundrel, but Vesper took the opportunity to satisfy her curiosity regarding at least one matter.

"Which did you think of first?" she asked. "Taking revenge on us or ruining Brazil?"

"Both at the same time, Miss Holly," replied Helvitius. "That is to say, the occasion of your Centennial brought all my plans immediately into focus. It was an opportunity that could not be ignored."

Vesper said no more. After a while, Helvitius grew uneasy, though he tried to conceal it. He drummed his fingers on the tabletop and hummed passages from *Rigoletto.* Finally, giving way to impatience, he had us all taken above decks, where he stood at the railing and gazed at the river. It was clear daylight, but neither Vesper nor I detected any sign of an approaching vessel.

"Should we be glad or sorry?" Vesper whispered. "I wish they could help, but I don't want them trapped along with us."

It occurred to me that we might have been mistaken. The boat which Vesper assumed to be following us might have been merely coincidental. My last view of The Weed had not been too encouraging; his only weapon, a pitiful stick from the pretzel cart. Assuming he fought free, it was more likely that he and the twins had returned to La Pierre House to set a new plan.

The same thought had come to Helvitius. He sighed and turned from the railing. "Your friends have disappointed me. It is no great matter. I shall prepare another letter for Dom Pedro. This time, I shall require Mrs. Garrett to deliver the documents."

"Fiend!" I cried. "How dare you involve the gentlest of beings in your foul scheme!"

"You might be sorry if you did," Vesper added. "Aunt Mary has her own score to settle with you. She hasn't forgotten you tried to kidnap her in Drackenberg."

"With your lives at stake," replied Helvitius, "I count on her obedience." He turned to Senhora Da Costa. "As for you, the moment has come to offer my heartfelt gratitude. You have accomplished your task, and have done so most excellently. Your services, dear lady, are no longer required. We have no further use for each other."

"Have we not?" retorted Senhora Da Costa. "You promised—"

"I promised that you would be avenged," Helvitius broke in. "Nothing beyond it. I have kept my word," he blandly went on. "You have helped set in motion a train of events which will avenge you a hundredfold. What more could you wish? You have been invaluable. Now, dear lady, I must dispense with you. Permanently."

It took a moment for the full significance of that final word to strike Senhora Da Costa. After an instant of puzzled disbelief, her face turned white with rage.

"You must appreciate my position," Helvitius continued. "It would be imprudence, even folly, to permit you to live, knowing what you know. You have my sincerest regrets. However—"

"Serpent!" With a cry, she seized the revolver from her purse, aimed the weapon at Helvitius, and fired.

When discharging a firearm, a cool head and a steady hand are essential for accuracy. Senhora Da Costa had neither. Her fury spoiled her aim, even at a target as large as Helvitius. The shot, alas, merely ripped through the sleeve of his dressing gown. Before she could pull the trigger again, the lascars sprang upon her. Vesper, quick though she was, found no chance for us to dart away in the momentary confusion. Several of the crew immediately surrounded us. Helvitius calmly picked up the revolver the lascars had torn from her hand and gave Senhora Da Costa an icy smile.

"Dear lady, we have nothing more to discuss." He smoothed his attire and made a curt motion with his head in the direction of the riverside. He snapped a command in Malay. The terrible lascars dragged Senhora Da Costa, still hissing curses and useless threats of revenge, down the gangplank. Where they conducted her I did not see, for I turned my face away in horror. Despite our previous encounters, the villain's ruthlessness never ceased to astonish and appall me. Vesper could only regard him with helpless outrage.

"Take that as an example." Helvitius narrowed his eyes at us. For all his show of aplomb, the attempt on his life had dampened his expansive mood. "The stakes are too high, Miss Holly, to dawdle with you. Do not doubt the seriousness of my goal. I shall stop at nothing to achieve it."

"You never did," retorted Vesper.

At that, Helvitius ordered the sailors to remove us from the yacht. I feared he intended for us to share the doom of Senhora Da Costa. Instead, they marched us down the pier to the freight yard and bolted us into a tin-roofed outbuilding. Even in this cheerless pen, prey to the unforeseeable miseries Helvitius held in store, Vesper's ever-compassionate thoughts went to Senhora Da Costa.

"Poor woman," Vesper murmured. "Revenge cost more than she figured. Brinnie—no matter what, I'm sorry for her."

Without wishing to appear less than sympathetic, I suggested that Senhora Da Costa had been a thoroughgoing villainess. Even so, I had to agree, the unhappy creature did not deserve such a dire end.

"What did she know?" Vesper wondered, as she now began to examine our place of captivity. "The whole scheme, I'd guess, whatever it is. I can see why Helvitius would get rid of her. I still can't see why he's so anxious for the documents. They're useless if Dom Pedro cancels them. Which he'll do. That bothered me back at La Pierre House. It keeps on bothering me.

"And what's Helvitius done with Januaria and Paulo?

Not available? What did he mean? They aren't aboard the *Minotaur,* I'd bet on that."

Our eyes, by now, had grown used to the dimness. Not that there was anything of interest to see. The empty structure might once have served as a toolshed or storage building. Vesper paced back and forth across the dirt floor. I could observe little of her face, but her voice had a most uncustomary tone of doubt.

"Brinnie, I've made a mess of it this time. Nothing's worked the way I calculated. We're worse off now than when we started. What should I have done? Anything would have been better."

It pained me to hear the dear girl reproach herself so bitterly. I told her that any plan might well have led to the same end. I urged her to turn her attention from the past to the present: namely, to devise a means of escape. Vesper resents being locked up and usually makes every strenuous effort to regain her freedom. Her answer, therefore, surprised me.

"Do we want to escape? Or stay where we are?" She left off her pacing and came to my side. "I'm sure Weed and the twins were in that boat. If they come looking for us and we aren't here, we can't help them or warn them.

"I still haven't any idea what Helvitius is up to, or what he's done with the children. How can I find out? Brinnie, I don't know what we should do."

It seemed preferable, I told her, to be out of the villain's clutches rather than in them. Vesper finally agreed. The question of escape, however, was purely academic. The shed offered no resources.

"Here's a bucket." Vesper had come upon the battered receptacle in a corner. I could imagine no possible value for such an item. Still, it cheered me to see that she had given up blaming herself and had recovered her usual enterprising spirit.

She knelt and scraped at the dirt floor. "There's one chance."

"Dear girl," I protested, "you can't think of digging our way out."

"Not exactly." Vesper hastily filled the bucket with loose earth. Once the container was packed to the brim, she hefted it and swung it back and forth. "That should be heavy enough."

She went and put her eye to the crack at the bottom of the door. "There's a guard. I see his feet. If I could take a good swipe at him— We'll have to get him in here first."

Motioning me to stand back, Vesper pounded on the door. "Are you going to starve us? We haven't eaten. We're hungry and thirsty."

This was true. Helvitius had not even offered us breakfast.

Though Vesper can be persuasive, her continued pleas and angry demands brought no response. At last, she stopped and seated herself on the ground, the bucket next to her.

"Somebody has to come in sooner or later. We'll wait. Be ready for them, Brinnie."

Vesper's entreaties finally did produce a result. Not long after, there came a sound of scuffling outside. The bolt was drawn and Vesper jumped to her feet, makeshift weapon in hand.

The sudden glare as the door flung open dazzled me a moment. Vesper had gripped the bucket, about to swing it against our guard. As he stepped inside, I glimpsed only a figure in headcloth and sarong: one of the infamous lascars.

The dear girl has a powerful arm. She halted in midswing, however. Fortunately.

"Carrots?"

The Weed sprang to her side.

"Are you all right?" He turned to me. "How are you, sir?"

Where and how he had obtained this garb, I could not imagine, but this was not the moment to speculate on his attire. He practically threw us bodily out the door and sent us stumbling into the freight yard.

"Come on! Fast!" The Weed, sarong flapping, sprinted in the direction of the railway siding.

Recovering a little from my astonishment, it now struck me that all my reservations about him were confirmed. Scholar he might be, but he was a rash, unthinking, incautious idiot. To liberate us, of all times, in broad daylight, with some of the *Minotaur*'s crew lounging along the pier and others clustered at a cook fire by one of the warehouses! The sight of a long-legged galloping lascar followed by two prisoners was more than enough to arouse suspicions. Within moments, shouting the alarm, the crewmen raced after us.

"There! Go!" The Weed gestured toward a rail spur. Smiler and Slider, urgently beckoning, crouched on the open platform of a handcar.

We scrambled aboard. The twins frantically pumped the long handles that set the vehicle in motion. Rusty from disuse, it creaked and groaned. The muscular pair bent all their strength to the task. As we gained speed, the crewmen doubled their efforts to overtake us. Helvitius, by now, had been alerted. I heard his voice furiously bellowing orders.

The platform barely had room for us all. We held on as best we could, risking being brained by the seesawing handles. Our progress, at least, was more rapid than that of our pursuers. We were on smooth tracks, while they stumbled along the railbed.

Our advantage was also our disadvantage. The handcar was obliged to follow the rail line, we could not veer from that set course. Also, human strength has its limits. Even with all of us taking turns pumping, we faced eventual exhaustion.

The Weed had enough intelligence to realize this. As we rounded a bend, momentarily out of sight of the crew, he pointed inland.

"Jump! Follow me!"

Vesper and the twins sprang from the handcar; I leaped after them. The rail line, I suddenly saw, had been laid along a sort of causeway, and I went scrambling and rolling down the slope.

The Weed plunged ahead: not toward solid ground but into boggy terrain. The fool was leading us into the wetlands of the Schuylkill.

For a time, we were able to lurch from one relatively firm piece of ground to another. The farther we headed into the marshes, the spongier grew the patches of earth. Tall cattails and reeds, rank outgrowths of swamp grass rose around us.

"They don't know which way we've gone," panted The Weed, as we dared to halt an instant in waist-high water. "They'll have to divide up."

"Right," Vesper agreed, with a glance of something like admiration at The Weed. "We'll only have to deal with half of them."

That still seemed an ample number. I already heard some of our pursuers crashing through the vegetation. The Weed ordered us to set off again. We floundered after him. The edge of the swamp lay not far ahead, but the clumps of reeds grew more sparsely there. Helvitius and his crew could hardly fail to sight us if we crawled out.

The Weed stopped and began plucking at the longest reeds, examining them, casting some aside until he collected a handful that suited him.

"Here." He handed one to each of us. "Duck under the water. Breath through this.

"An old Lenni-Lenape trick, sir," he assured me as I looked doubtfully at him. "I tried it once. Really, it works."

Vesper and the twins, unquestioning, had already plunged below the surface.

"Just don't chew on the end," The Weed advised, as he disappeared under the water.

I forced myself to sink into the muddy, foul-smelling liquid, gulping air through the hollow reed. I could not estimate how long I remained there, with brackish water filling my nose and ears. It seemed forever. Lying motionless and submerged was probably second nature to the Lenni-Lenape. For anyone else, it required getting used to. Yet, The Weed was right. I did manage to breathe—not easily, but enough to keep from drowning.

Until my reed collapsed.

CHAPTER

❧ 10 ❧

To come to the surface and reveal our hiding place or
to remain on the bottom and discontinue breathing for the
foreseeable future presented a difficult choice. I did not
have to make the decision. As I pondered the best course,
choking and thrashing about in ooze, Vesper became
aware of my plight. Before my lungs burst, I was hauled
gasping from that fetid pool, Vesper and The Weed sup-
porting me on either side.

Between them, they dragged me to slightly more solid
ground. As Vesper helped me dispose of the brackish
water I had unintentionally gulped down, The Weed knelt
beside me.

"Are you all right, sir?"

Apparently, I replied, I was.

"Good for you, sir. They've gone," he added.
"They've passed us by or headed the other way."

Smiler and Slider, by now, had crawled from the pool
none the worse for wear. Vesper was as bedraggled as I

had ever seen her. The Weed had lost his headcloth, tendrils of swamp grass garlanded his dripping hair. They looked more like a pair of ancient barbarians than Philadelphians.

The Weed stripped off the sarong that had concealed his rolled-up canvas trousers. The twins shook themselves like water spaniels. Though physically sopping wet, their spirits were undampened.

"We've been in worse," remarked Smiler. "Slider and I spent some bad moments in a hot sulfur spring, out in the Territories. A posse wanted to discuss a misunderstanding about a couple of absent horses, but we thought it was better to avoid the subject."

"We came out parboiled, as you might say," added Slider. "Here at least the water's cool."

Vesper, meanwhile, glanced hastily around. Sure that Helvitius and his hirelings had lost us for the moment, she set off toward higher, drier ground. With his lanky legs, The Weed matched her stride for stride as the twins and I lurched along behind. Even in the screen of underbrush, we continued at a rapid pace, hoping to put as much distance between ourselves and our pursuers.

At one point, when Vesper appeared uncertain which direction to follow, The Weed stepped confidently ahead. Indeed, he moved as quickly and silently as a shadow. I had seen only one person track so swiftly and surely: Acharro, chief of the Chirica tribe in El Dorado. The Weed seemed perfectly at home here. I wondered if, at one point, some ancestral Passavants might have conjoined with the Lenni-Lenape.

Once we had left the wetlands far behind, Vesper slowed her pace: not to catch her breath—the dear girl is remarkably fit—but to satisfy her curiosity. She was eager to learn more of our timely rescue, not to mention the pretzel cart and The Weed's sarong.

"Sorry about the cart," said The Weed in reply to her questions. "I suppose I should have stayed where you told me. But I thought if I moved around I could keep a better eye on whatever happened. Then I ran into the pretzel man—old Joe, I've known him for years—and he let me use his cart."

"We're glad he did," put in Smiler. "Mr. Toby kept roaming about while we stayed put. He's the one who saw you with the dockers and the governess."

"I didn't think it was part of the plan," said The Weed. "Things just didn't look right to me."

"They weren't," said Vesper. "To begin with, Senhora Da Costa wasn't a governess." She quickly described the wretched woman's treachery and our abduction.

"We never would have thought that of her." The Weed shook his head. "All we could tell, they were taking you downriver and you didn't want to go. A friend of mine has a couple of steam launches at the waterfront. He was glad to lend us one, no questions asked.

"We followed until we had a notion where you were going, then we beached the boat and tracked you from the shore. By the time we reached the yacht they were hauling you off to the shed. We'd have come after you then if it hadn't been for Senhora Da Costa."

"You saw her?" I exclaimed. "Murdered in cold blood!"

"Oh, no, sir," said The Weed. "She's alive. In a pretty bad temper, though."

"They'd have done her in for certain if we hadn't been

watching from the bushes," added Slider. "Mr. Toby couldn't stand by and do nothing. So we all pitched in."

"Mr. Toby did most of it," Smiler said. "We've never seen anyone like him for grabbing and punching. Slider and I mainly tied up and gagged those fellows in skirts. Mr. Toby took the clothes from one of them. We got their knives"—he pointed to the dagger in his belt and Slider did likewise—"we thought they might come in handy."

"Well done," said Vesper. "I only wish we could have got hold of Senhora Da Costa. She knows what Helvitius is up to."

"Too late now," The Weed said. "She ran off as fast as she could while we were busy with the lascars. I can't say I blame her."

The disappearance of Senhora Da Costa interested me less than our own liberation.

"Not much to tell about that, sir," The Weed replied. "The guard at the shed thought I was one of the crew. By the time he realized I wasn't— I'm afraid he'll have a bad headache when he wakes up."

Vesper beamed him an admiring glance, much impressed by his modest account. I had never pictured The Weed as an expert at fisticuffs. Yet, observing him hunkered down with his back against a tree, I saw him less mantislike and more primitive. There had been the occasional glint in his eye indicating that fighting was not entirely distasteful to him. I preferred him in his scholarly aspect.

The Weed shrugged off Vesper's gratitude and praise. "The main thing, you're well away from Helvitius. But— you know him better than I do. What's he likely to try next?"

"No way to guess," replied Vesper. "All we can do is

keep clear of him. We don't dare go back and get your boat. How can we reach Dom Pedro? On foot? That's too long a walk in the open, with Helvitius and his crew on the loose.

"Shall we go to Strafford?" Vesper went on. "It's closer than Philadelphia. We'd be safer at home, and we could send word to Dom Pedro. By now he's wondering what became of us. Aunt Mary must be wondering the same."

Eager though I was to be with my angelic Mary, I reminded Vesper that from here to Strafford hardly counted as an easy ramble. In the best circumstances, it would take a couple of days or more of walking. And we were without food, shelter, or friends along the way.

"All right," said Vesper, "I have a better idea. First, we head for Aronimink."

"Those dreadful backlands?" I exclaimed. Unlike the genteel meadows of Strafford, Aronimink had remained barely touched by the civilizing influence of Philadelphia.

"Not as bad as all that, sir," said The Weed. "I used to play explorer there. Marvelous rock formations. The Drexel Hills, of course. And Indian Basin."

"I'm thinking of someone who can help us," Vesper said. "Maybe lend us a carriage or horses. Or get word to Aunt Mary to come and fetch us."

I could imagine no such benefactor, least of all in the wilds of Aronimink.

"General Gallaway," said Vesper. "Dapper Dan. Remember? Sam Grant called him one of his best officers. He has a farm there. It's our best chance."

The more I considered, the more I realized that Vesper was correct, as usual. What better sanctuary than with a gallant comrade-in-arms of the president himself? My spirits rose—until it occurred to me that Aronimink was, nevertheless, a good distance away.

"We can do it," Vesper assured me. "We'll keep going as long as we can, hole up for the night, and be there tomorrow."

With that, we set off northward. Vesper, however, might have been a shade too optimistic regarding our progress. The natural beauties of our commonwealth are unrivaled, but the path to Aronimink was not one of them. Nor should I refer to it as a path. The increasingly dense undergrowth offered us not so much as the vestige of a trail, let alone any kind of backcountry road. Despite our best efforts, a moonless night fell upon us before we had trudged halfway to our destination.

Smiler and Slider did their best to arrange a shelter from dead branches and piles of leaves: more like a beaver lodge than anything else. The twins, able to make themselves comfortable on a bed of nails, curled up and were soon cheerfully snoring in identical cadences. The Weed sat cross-legged, staring gloomily into the darkness.

Poor fellow, I could only sympathize. For all his bounce and eagerness, the strain of past events had only now begun to take their toll on him: the pursuit downriver, his combat with venomous lascars, our narrow escape from Helvitius, and, as well, the prospect of hard travel yet in store.

Vesper went to his side and gently put a hand on his shoulder. "What's wrong, Toby?"

"Something worries me." He turned a most woebegone face to her. "It could be a mistake."

"Aronimink? What better—"

"Not that." The Weed sighed miserably. "The beans. If I made a mistake translating that part of the inscription, the whole thing could be wrong."

The two of them began an intense discussion of Minoan hieroglyphics. I pulled my jacket over my head and tried my best to sleep.

At first light, Vesper was up and impatient to be on our way. Without implying any criticism of her, I must say the dear girl had grown more familiar with remote corners of the world than with our Pennsylvania localities. While she knew the general direction of Aronimink, she gladly turned over the guidance of our disheveled band to The Weed, who led us as briskly as the rough terrain allowed.

It would have been a glorious Philadelphia May morning except for a spitefully chill wind from New Jersey. Clouds gathered overhead as thick as the brush underfoot. Before noon, rain bucketed down in such blinding sheets I could barely see Slider and Smiler trotting a few feet ahead.

The downpour stopped long enough for our clothing to turn from soaking wet to merely clammy, and thus continued throughout the afternoon. The Weed seemed impervious to water.

As we gained the crest of a wooded ridge, he halted a moment. "Just like Longfellow's 'Evangeline,' wouldn't you say? 'This is the forest primeval. The murmuring pines and the hemlocks, Bearded with moss and in garments green. . . .'"

He stood, hands on hips, scraggly head thrown back,

and flared his nostrils. I asked if he intended to sniff out Aronimink.

"But we're in Aronimink, sir," he replied. "Actually, have been for a while now. You can't really see where it begins and ends. You might even call it a geographical state of mind. I don't know the place, but I'd guess General Gallaway's farm is down there." He pointed toward a clumpy little valley this side of the looming Drexel Hills.

"Could be." Vesper's eyes followed his gesture. "There's a farm with a flagpole. Let's try that one. If we're wrong, whoever lives there can give us directions."

By the time we reached the bottomland, the rain came back to drench us again. Setting our course by the flagpole, we plodded up a muddy lane. Farm buildings lay at the end of it, beyond a rail fence and locked gate.

Vesper started to climb over this obstacle, then halted, perched on the rail. I saw the reason for her hesitation.

From a lean-to emerged a tall, lantern-jawed figure in a blue army jacket with faded sergeant's stripes. A slouch hat was pulled down on his head. What made Vesper pause was the carbine he aimed at us.

❧ 11 ❧

"We're looking for General Gallaway," Vesper said pleasantly, despite the carbine pointed at her.

"Clear off. All of you." The man directed his remark and his aim toward The Weed, who had approached the gate. "No trespassers."

"We aren't trespassing," said Vesper. "We have to see General Gallaway."

"General Dan sees nobody."

"He'll see us," replied Vesper. "We're friends of Sam Grant."

The man started at the name of his commander-in-chief, gave us a slantwise look, and finally lowered his weapon. "You just stay put."

He set off at a dogtrot for the main farm building. Vesper would have climbed over the gate and followed him, but I suggested heeding the sergeant, especially since he was armed. Also, as a high military officer, General Gallaway might take it amiss if five uninvited arrivals suddenly invaded him.

We stood uncomfortably some while before the sergeant returned to unlock the gate, then made our way into the farmyard. It was a pleasant enough little spread, with neatly kept stables, a barn, a carriage house. General Gallaway had apparently laid down the sword in favor of dairying and cattle breeding. Though its occupant was not visible at the moment, a bull pen stood further down the yard, a cowshed nearby. Whitewashed stones ringed the flagpole which had served as our guide.

The farmhouse was old and rambling. Some of the windows had been boarded up. Dripping and muddy, we crossed a wooden porch and entered the main room. Hands on hips, General Gallaway stood by a trestle table. He flashed a pair of diamond-bright blue eyes at us. I could not judge whether he was pleased or irritated.

He cast an appraising glance at Vesper, and she did likewise to him. I thought to myself that Dapper Dan Gallaway lived up to his nickname. His attire matched his renowned flamboyance: fringed buckskin jacket, officer's trousers tucked into tooled leather boots, a long-barreled revolver holstered at his belt, a cavalryman's yellow scarf around his neck. His famous golden ringlets—a little tarnished now—hung about his shoulders in jaunty disarray: an effect that must have taken careful study to achieve.

"Welcome to a simple soldier's billet, ma'am," said General Gallaway, after Vesper presented us. "Humble quarters, but you embellish them."

If Vesper's seafaring costume puzzled him, he ignored it. He kissed her hand with a smooth flourish that, in former days, would have brought on palpitations in every female heart and vexation in every male. Vesper smiled calmly.

"Sergeant Shote." Dapper Dan turned to his aide-de-camp, who still regarded us uneasily. "My compliments to Cook and ask her to get something delicious on the table for this lovely lady and her friends."

Trailing his carbine, Sergeant Shote vanished in the direction of the kitchen. Dapper Dan invited us to take places at the table.

"Now, then, ma'am, I'm honored by your presence but ignorant of your purpose. Friends of Sam Grant, you say? He should count himself fortunate, he has few of them these days."

Vesper tried to explain our situation as best she could, bearing in mind Grant's admonition of secrecy. The Weed took it on himself to interrupt.

"Sir, without putting too fine a point on it," he said, as I rolled my eyes heavenward, "it's a matter of life and death."

"Tut, tut, laddie," said General Gallaway, "not many things are as serious as that, and nothing the U.S. cavalry can't set right. If you want to talk life and death, talk about Cold Harbor. Talk about Antietam. Talk about Gettysburg."

As far as I knew, General Gallaway had not taken part in those engagements, but I understood his point. The Weed said no more as Vesper continued.

"We have to get to Strafford as soon as we can. Is there a carriage we can borrow? We'll return it, I promise you."

"Lovely lady, I would trust your word in all things.

Yes, I have an excellent carriage." General Gallaway's face fell. "Alas, I cannot put it at your disposal. The axle is broken, the damage beyond the ability even of Sergeant Shote to repair. I am presently awaiting the arrival of a blacksmith. Thus far, he has not chosen to attend on me. The attitude of tradesmen these days, need I tell you, is insufferable."

"Is there any way we can send a message?" asked Vesper.

Dapper Dan nodded. "Of course, ma'am. I shall dispatch one of the hired hands or Sergeant Shote himself. He will be as honored to serve you as I am. Meantime, I offer you all the hospitality of this modest abode. Spare rooms are available—small comfort, ma'am, but they are yours."

Vesper thanked him for his kindness, but urged him to send a messenger immediately. General Gallaway shook his head.

"There is no use in it. In this weather?" The rain, indeed, had begun worse than ever, dashing against the roof and windows like volleys of grapeshot. "The roads would be impassable. The Darby Creek, I have no doubt, is already at flood level. It will subside; we shall have a truce in this battle of the elements. Whatever your mission, dear lady, it will not be compromised by a few hours' delay."

The prospect of any delay whatever did not sit well with Vesper. General Gallaway, however, had no more immediate help to offer. Nor could we continue on foot, at night, in such a downpour. As for the general himself, though he had chosen a rustic retreat in the wilds of Aronimink, he was not displeased to entertain an unexpected guest like Vesper. He settled expansively in his chair, affording us a clear view of that profile once known to every reader of *Harper's Weekly* and the newspaper press.

By then, the cook and Sergeant Shote had come bearing refreshment trays. We received them gladly. And I confess that, bone weary as I was, an obligatory night's sleep attracted me, all the more since we had no other choice.

"Sam Grant would have come by to see you," remarked Vesper, by way of table talk. "He'll do it another time."

The dear girl seldom, if ever, says a wrong or tactless word. In this case, I feared that she did. General Gallaway's face clouded. Grant had praised his brother officer, but, I recalled, he had also mentioned differences and fallings-out, perhaps more serious than he chose to admit.

"Another time is a time too late," General Gallaway retorted. "Does he think to patronize me now? *President* Grant? Had it not been for his conniving, that office would be mine. I should have won the nomination in 1868. Grant and his cronies stole and swindled me out of it. Just as Honest Abe—Honest Ape, more like it—stole the election from General McClellan."

Vesper frowned at the simian reference. Personally, I was grateful that McClellan had lost to Mr. Lincoln of honored memory. On the other hand, McClellan was a Philadelphian.

Caught up in his subject, Gallaway pressed on. "Has Grant confirmed me in my rank? I remain a brevet general, a temporary grade. He promised me a Western command. Has he given it to me? No. Indeed, I hear talk that he intends to appoint that incompetent idiot George Custer, with his Seventh Cavalry band tooting 'Garryowen.' Can you see that fancy fool campaign against marauding redskins? He has his eye on the presidency, but, by Heaven, he will not gain it.

"Six years ago, I offered my services as adviser to Bismarck in Prussia. Politely declined! Grant's hand was in that, too. Who was chosen? A strutting bantam rooster: Sheridan. Little Phil! For his military genius? No, for the sake of that so-called ride!"

"Remarkable gallop, wouldn't you say?" The Weed blundered in. "Isn't there a poem? Yes, 'Sheridan's Ride.' How does it go? 'Up from the south, at break of day, Bringing to Winchester fresh dismay . . .' and something and something . . . 'Telling the battle was on once more, And Sheridan twenty miles away.' "

"Ten miles! Ten miles, if that!" Dapper Dan sprang to his feet. "Tom Read was a cheap versifier and a liar. I shall deal with him in my memoirs. No, sir, if anything that line should be: And *Gallaway* twenty miles away!"

The general's bright eyes darted back and forth; he had grown so agitated over his grievances that I wondered if he might be a little mad. With high military officers, it is not easy to tell.

He regained better command of himself and sat down, though still noticeably unsettled. He fixed a glance on Vesper. "Far be it from me to speak ill of one you consider a friend, but honesty compels me. Grant is not fit for his high office. He has lost the military virtues, the soldier's honor and fidelity. In short, ma'am, he has become—a civilian."

Dapper Dan fell silent. His outburst had left him

somewhat disheveled. His carefully arranged ringlets had mutinied and hung every which way. Finally, he wished us an abrupt good-night. We left him glooming at the empty fireplace as Sergeant Shote led us to our quarters.

Smiler and Slider were obliged to occupy the stables. General Gallaway had not been over-modest when he spoke of small comfort. The Weed was consigned to a room about the size of a linen closet. Vesper and I did not fare much better. Our chamber held little more than a cot and a bureau, to which Sergeant Shote added a rickety camp bed.

"I wish we hadn't stopped," Vesper told me. "Dapper Dan's no friend of Sam Grant. Tomorrow, rain or shine, if he doesn't send word to Aunt Mary, I say we move on."

I made myself as comfortable as possible, given the tendency of my camp bed to lurch at every move. The rain, at least, had stopped drumming on the roof. I drifted off to sleep, but at dawn Vesper roused me and drew me to the window.

"Sergeant Shote. Dapper Dan." She pointed down. In the half light, I made out the sergeant's figure on horseback, attentively listening to orders from his commanding officer.

I gave a sigh of relief. Dapper Dan had kept his promise, dispatching his aide-de-camp on an early gallop to Strafford.

"I hope he rides as fast as Sheridan," said Vesper.

So did I. In happy anticipation of rejoining my dear Mary, perhaps before the day ended, I closed my eyes again. Soon after, what sounded like hailstones rattled the window. Vesper beckoned to me. Slider—or Smiler—had been tossing pebbles. Seeing us awake, he gestured for us to come down.

We quickly left our room. Passing by The Weed's cubbyhole, Vesper peered in. The Weed was standing in his Gond posture—for all I knew, he could have spent the night in that meditative attitude. Leaving him undisturbed, we hurried downstairs. Dapper Dan had either gone back to bed or had closeted himself with his memoirs. The farmyard was empty and silent.

"Now, here's a strange piece of business," Slider told us as we headed for the carriage house. "We didn't notice it until we woke up when that sergeant fellow saddled his horse."

"Seeing as how General Dan couldn't get his carriage mended," said Smiler, "we thought we'd do him a favor and fix it. There's not much Slider and I can't put right in the vehicular line."

"Then," added Slider, "it turned out we didn't need to. Broken axle? Miss Vesper, that carriage is good as new. Not a thing wrong with it. You see for yourself."

To me, it was clear enough. Dapper Dan simply did not wish to lend his carriage despite his expressed willingness. The military virtues apparently did not include generosity.

"That's not all of it," said Slider. "While we were looking at the carriage, diagnosing the ailment, in a manner of speaking, we found this on the floor."

He held out a small-sized article of flat-topped headgear with a red pom-pom, a sailor's hat that young boys delight to wear in imitation of their elders. Vesper studied the lettering around the headband.

"*Marinha do Brasil,*" she said. "The Brazilian Navy."

❧ 12 ❧

Vesper turned the hat around and around in her hands, thoughtfully studying it. The twins watched silently, their faces filled with identical apprehension.

"So, that's it," Vesper said, after a moment. "Dapper Dan's in the scheme."

The idea was too monstrous. General Gallaway, at present, might well be something of a madman, but there was no denying his past heroism, and certainly, a ranking officer of our Grand Army of the Republic would never conspire with an archfiend like Helvitius. I grasped at any straw to explain the unexplainable. Perhaps the hat was a souvenir, military men have the habit of collecting all sorts of paraphernalia. He might have bought it, or received it as a gift. True, it appeared to be a boy's headgear, but it could have belonged to a very small sailor.

"It has Paulo's name inside," Vesper said, shattering all those possibilities.

"Sergeant Shote?" I suggested. "A villain if ever I've seen one."

"Dapper Dan gives the orders," Vesper said. "Shote only obeys them. I don't see how else it could be. Senhora Da Costa told some of the truth. The children were hauled off in a carriage. This carriage. They weren't aboard the *Minotaur* for a good reason: They're here."

"Then we must confront General Gallaway," I declared. "Face him down, bring him to account for this evil conspiracy—as such it must be."

"Last thing in the world we'll do," Vesper countered. "If he knows that we know— Brinnie, that's even worse trouble for us."

In that case, I urged, we should depart immediately.

"Not yet," said Vesper. "I'm assuming Dapper Dan's keeping the children on the farm. Locked away—but where? We have to find them and get them out. We can't go dashing off and leave them."

What then, I asked, did she suggest?

"Breakfast," said Vesper. "As if nothing happened. After that, we'll see. I don't think we have much time. Sergeant Shote's been long on his way. Not to Strafford, that's for sure. Unless I miss my guess, Dapper Dan sent him straight to Helvitius. We don't know what they'll do about us. As for what we'll do about them—"

Vesper had no opportunity to continue her speculation. We had only set foot outside the carriage house when she halted.

General Gallaway stood in our path.

"Awake before reveille, dear lady?" The general looked as if he himself had not slept all night, with his fringes tangled and his ringlets in complete disorder. "I have been observing you from my window. You would have done well to keep to your quarters."

Vesper attempted to hide Paulo's hat beneath her jacket. Too late, for General Gallaway had already noted that item of damning evidence. A trumped-up excuse would have been futile, so Vesper offered none.

"Where are the children?" she demanded.

In reply, General Gallaway drew his long-barreled revolver. Various individuals had been pointing firearms at us for the past couple of days; now this, from a former national hero, could not go uncriticized.

"You disgrace your rank and the uniform you gallantly wore," I flung at him. "You, sir, have connived with the greatest villain blighting our world. Have you fallen so low? To consort, to conspire with that abominable wretch?"

"If you refer to Dr. Helvitius, Professor Garrett, you are mistaken in your opinion. He is a man of rare vision, sir, and the widest ranging views. He has a soldier's enterprise and initiative. Civilian though he is, I, sir, salute him. Had he chosen the profession of arms, he would be the Napoleon of our day."

"At Waterloo, I hope," said Vesper.

"He speaks highly of you," replied General Gallaway. "He is one of your admirers—up to the point where you interfere with his activities, as you have so often done. Yes, lovely lady, he has discussed you at length. I never expected to meet you in person. Your arrival here was not part of his grand design. What he will propose to do with you— We can only await him and learn that.

"Meantime, I regret you must be confined to quarters"—General Gallaway motioned with the revolver— "so please oblige me by lying down. My men will see to your accommodations."

Outnumbered as he was, the general took this precaution to render us prone and helpless while he removed his neckerchief and signaled to a couple of hired hands already working in the nearby pasture.

Sprawled flat as I was on the muddy ground, with General Gallaway threatening me whenever I ventured to raise my head, I could not see if the hired men perceived his signal. What I could not see, however, I could hear. It struck me, at first, as one of Mr. Baldwin's powerful locomotives bearing down on us with a furious bellowing and puffing and the pounding of mighty pistons.

General Gallaway shouted in angry astonishment. Daring a glance, I saw the gate of the bull pen had flung open, and its occupant, an enormous black beast, was charging toward us at top speed.

Head lowered, horns pointed straight at General Gallaway, the bull roared and snorted, thundering across the farmyard.

At the flank of this infuriated creature, whooping and guiding it along, raced The Weed.

When last seen, The Weed had been folded into his peaceful Gond attitude. Now his eyes blazed as fiercely as the bull's. The sight of the galloping Weed must have been as alarming to General Gallaway as the bull itself. An experienced commander, General Gallaway should have been used to unforeseen events. This time, however, he was torn between keeping his revolver trained on his captives, summoning aid, and avoiding impalement on the terrible horns. His waving neckerchief only increased the bull's frenzy.

General Gallaway chose to face the most immediate

danger. He spun around and tried to level his revolver. Before he could fire, the bull was nearly upon him. As The Weed sprang aside, Gallaway threw himself out of the path of this four-legged projectile and made for the shelter of the carriage house. The creature pursued him even there, with subsequent crashing noises.

Vesper needed no other opportunity. She was on her feet in an instant. I scrambled out of the mud and, The Weed and the twins beside me, streaked after her. We pelted across a rutted field, tumbled over a fence, and sped into the dense undergrowth.

Vesper is experienced in making quick departures over difficult country; The Weed had claimed boyhood knowledge of the Aronimink wilderness. Therefore, when we halted and Vesper told The Weed of our discovery, I was dismayed to realize we had merely circled the farm without going any great distance from it. Could Vesper, with her unfailing sense of direction, have so badly misjudged?

"No," she said. "Why go far if we only have to go back? The children are there. They must be. I want to get them."

I, too, was convinced that General Gallaway was holding Paulo and Januaria captive; but, I reminded Vesper, Helvitius would by now have been alerted. He or his ruffians could arrive perhaps within an hour or two.

"Exactly," said Vesper. "We have to do it now."

"That's right, sir," The Weed put in. "It's our best chance. *Occasionem cognoscere,* recognize the opportunity, wouldn't you say?"

I recognized a marvelous opportunity to leave hastily, but in the discussion that followed, Smiler and Slider were willing to take the risk. For the moment, as Vesper told us, we would keep our hiding place until General Gallaway was on our trail.

"What?" I exclaimed. "Wait until he finds us?"

"Until he starts looking for us," replied Vesper. "Then we double back to the farm. We'll have time. Not much, but there can't be too many places to search. Nobody's in the carriage house, or Smiler and Slider would have seen them. The barn? Not likely. The doors were wide open. That leaves the stables, the outbuildings, and the farmhouse. We'll divide up. With four of us looking—"

"Five," corrected The Weed.

"Four," said Vesper. "I don't know if it's too risky, but if you can keep Dapper Dan beating the bushes for us, we'll have a free hand at the farm. I'm not sure I like the idea, though. If he catches up with you—"

"He won't," declared The Weed. "I'll lead him a chase. Just as we used to play hare and hounds."

The Weed's eyes lit up, and he grinned like an overgrown boy. I had the feeling he actually enjoyed the prospect. I reminded him we were not playing games. He had never dealt with the diabolical cunning of Helvitius.

"But you have, sir," he said. "You'll be fine."

I thanked him for that assurance. The Weed now pointed toward the Drexel Hills. If we took our bearings from the highest peak, he told us, and headed north, we would strike the tall rock formation of Indian Basin. He would meet us there.

"If—well, if I'm unavoidably delayed," he added, "you'll think of something."

Our course of action decided, Vesper brought up the matter of General Gallaway's bull. The Weed explained that he had seen our predicament, run from the house, and released the creature.

"It was the first thing that came to mind," he said. When I suggested that, in rescuing us, he had put us in a good way of being gored or trampled, The Weed firmly shook his head. "No trouble handling a bull, sir. If you have the knack. I tried it before, in Crete. The Minoans used to do bull-dancing, I saw the old vase paintings. You mainly need to have a way with animals."

A way with animals was indeed a remarkable gift. Zoltan, king of the Gypsies in Drackenberg, possessed it, but I never expected to find it in a Philadelphia Passavant.

The bull must have been recaptured, for we could hear, a short distance away, the sound of crashing underbrush and the occasional angry command from General Gallaway.

The Weed, in his role of hare, sprang up and headed in the direction of the general and his hired hands, who by now had come to his assistance.

If Vesper had any second thoughts about her plan, it was too late to reconsider. With the sounds of pursuit fading behind us, we plunged through the bushes and raced to the farm. In the empty yard, Vesper instructed Smiler and Slider to investigate the outbuildings. In the house itself, she would search the attic and cellar; and I, the first floor rooms.

We separated. Vesper raced upstairs. In the main room, I saw no likely place of captivity. I turned my attention to the kitchen, pantry, and adjoining washhouse. Alas,

I overlooked one detail which threatened to end my search then and there: General Gallaway's cook.

The good woman, when I burst into the kitchen, was kneading bread on a wooden table. At sight of me, she screamed at the top of her voice and flung the batch of dough at my head with surprising accuracy. Still shrieking, she snatched up the rolling pin.

I raised my hands to ward off the blow, at the same time assuring the desperate cook that I meant her no harm. Instead of striking me, she scrambled to the pantry door and set her back against it. This protective attitude made me suspect there was more in the general's larder than the general's victuals.

"Madam, if you please—" I gestured for her to stand away and shouted for Vesper. Ignoring my soothing tone, the cook set about belaboring me with the rolling pin.

Though it goes against my disposition and my principles to treat one of the gentler sex with anything less than courtesy, in view of the blows raining upon my head, I had to exercise firmness in removing her from her guard post.

Fending off her continued attack, I kicked vigorously at the pantry door. At last, it splintered. I heaved the cook aside and plunged in.

A dark-haired, slender lad in a sailor suit was on his feet by the far shelves of the pantry, beside him, a girl with honey-colored ringlets and a cherubic little face.

In her charming pinafore, ribbons in her tresses, infantile innocence glowing from her delicate features, this angelic being—I could see her in no other terms—cried out and ran toward me.

"Unhappy child!" I declared. "Have no fear, you shall be free of this dreadful prison."

I held out my arms to her.

She kicked me in the shins.

CHAPTER

❧ 13 ❧

My dear Mary can determine a child's age at a single
glance. I do not have this ability, beyond perceiving one
individual to be larger than another. I could only guess
vaguely that Januaria might be somewhere between three
and five. Such vigor from one of so few years astonished
me, all the more as she continued her attack on my shins.

As for Paulo, I was too occupied with his sister to do
more than reckon him, roughly, to be perhaps eight or
nine. But he was a manly little fellow. He boldly advanced
on me, fists upraised, and began pummeling me with all
his might.

What with the cook screaming and belaboring me, the
youngsters assaulting me and, at the same time, howling
and yelling enough to burst their little lungs, I thought it
best to withdraw. By then, however, Vesper had arrived
in answer to my shouts. Smiler and Slider, drawn by the
racket, joined us in the kitchen.

"The poor things are upset," I explained.

Vesper waited for no further details. She snatched up the kicking and wriggling Januaria. Smiler seized Paulo in his burly arms. Slider, as rear guard, defended us against the cook, at last flinging her into the washhouse. He joined us as we raced out of the farmyard as fast as I could limp.

We plunged into the woodlands. Exhausted by their struggles against what they must have taken for yet another kidnapping, the children fell silent except for the occasional yell from little Januaria. Vesper halted long enough to transfer her angelic burden to the custody of Slider, then loped ahead to take her bearings from the peak of the Drexel Hills.

Brambles tore at us, we stumbled over the roots of the ancient Aronimink trees. With saplings whipping at my face, I kept on blindly, trusting the dear girl's sense of direction. After some while, she slowed, then waved us toward a high outcropping of bare rocks.

"Indian Basin. There it is." She stepped into a little clearing. The configuration of rocks bore a wide and deep cleft a few feet from the ground. The upper shelf dripped moisture; the lower held a moss-fringed indentation, indeed much like a large and shallow basin.

Vesper glanced around, listening carefully. Her keen ears detected no sounds of pursuit. The Weed, presumably, had been a successful hare. However, there was no sign of him.

"We'll meet him here," said Vesper. "That's what he told us. We'll wait."

I had no chance to raise the obvious questions: How long? What next? No sooner had the twins set the chil-

dren on the turf than Paulo darted from the clearing, little
Januaria pelting after him.

The children, quick though they were, offered no challenge to Vesper's long legs. She sprinted off like an ante-
lope and caught up with them in a matter of moments.
Seeing himself overtaken, Paulo seized a dead branch and
set his back to a tree. Despite this peculiar behavior, he
was a brave lad and a cool one. He seemed quite ready to
sell his life dearly. Had he been a dozen years older, I
would have kept my distance from him.

He tightened his grip on the makeshift weapon. His
eyes flashed as he looked squarely at Vesper. His dark
curls clung damply to his brow; his face held a look of ear-
nest intensity. Januaria crouched beside him, her arms
wrapped around one of his legs.

"Shall you kill us now?" he demanded.

"Klissnao?" echoed little Januaria.

Vesper blinked at him. "Paulo, what are you talking
about?"

"You are the bad people coming to kill us," retorted
Paulo. "We know. That is why we were taken away, so
you do not find us. Senhora Da Costa told us."

"That evil creature?" I exclaimed. "That wretch! That
villainess!"

I went on to explain that their false governess had be-
trayed them, that she was ruthless, vengeful, and not at all
a good person.

Little Januaria burst into tears.

"We like Senhora Da Costa." Paulo raised his chin.
"She is nice to us. We want her."

I could not believe my ears. Not only had Senhora Da

Costa conspired with Helvitius, she had, as well, managed to steal the affection of these innocent babes.

"Brinnie, don't you see what's happened? The children have been lied to. They thought they were being taken away for their own safety. That made it easier to kidnap them. They wouldn't fuss; they'd behave themselves. Much better than tying them up and having to guard them every moment. They wouldn't try to escape, either."

Vesper turned back to Paulo and Januaria. Speaking in Portuguese, she patiently explained what, in truth, had been the case. Few, if any, have been able to resist Vesper at her most persuasive. By the time she finished, Paulo put down his dead branch. He and Januaria gazed at her with something close to devoted adoration, as many of their elders had done. The twins had come to join us, and the sight of their honest, forthright faces doubly convinced the little ones.

"Fessagat?" said Januaria, after Vesper introduced me and Paulo had solemnly shaken my hand.

"Professor Garrett," repeated Vesper. "Brinnie. You can call him 'Uncle Brinnie' if you like."

"Oncabinni?" Januaria beamed, forgiving me for having frightened her and excusing me for obliging her to kick my shins.

Vesper, so far, had continued the conversation in Portuguese. Paulo now interrupted her to declare proudly that he could speak English.

"Senhora Da Costa was also starting to teach English to my sister," said Paulo. With a smile of superiority, he added, "But she is not learning very much. She does not speak so well as I."

"Dutu!" protested Januaria. "Spikinglish."

In proof thereof, the adorable cherub came out with a babble of words and phrases that were as inscrutable to me as The Weed's Minoan tablets.

Suddenly The Weed himself stood in the clearing. How he had come so silently I could not imagine, unless he was, in fact, part Lenni-Lenape. But there he was, leaning against the rocks of Indian Basin, his face a little flushed, his clothing a little torn, yet, all in all, looking pleased with himself.

"Found it?" he said. "Knew you would."

"Toby!" Vesper ran to embrace him enthusiastically, though he had not been gone all that long.

"Got them safe and sound? Bravo, all of you." The Weed grinned at the children. "Hello, youngsters. Let's have a look."

The Weed bent down and did one of the silliest things I had yet seen him do. He wiggled his ears. The children stared in fascination.

"They're fine now," said Vesper. "Brinnie may have a bruise or two."

Having accepted us as friends, Paulo made a very gentlemanly apology for his behavior. In answer to Vesper's questions, he talked eagerly about the abduction. Vesper's guess had been correct. Senhora Da Costa had indeed convinced the children that their lives were in danger. Believing that they were obeying the emperor's orders, they trustfully climbed into General Gallaway's carriage and were whisked off to the farm. These recollections no way distressed the children. I gathered that Paulo and Januaria had been well treated, given the run of the farm, and, in fact, were having a marvelous time. When we unexpectedly arrived, they were told to hide in the pantry. Bad people were coming to kill them, they must not make a sound.

"Biquat," explained little Januaria, which I took to signify "Be quiet."

"The youngsters were their own best guards and jailers," said The Weed. "Helvitius worked that out very cleverly. Yes, he's tricky, Carrots, I see what you mean. Well, now that we have them, what's to do?"

"I still think we should go to Strafford," said Vesper. "Not on foot. That's too long a tramp for Januaria and Paulo. First thing: We get out of Aronimink and into civilization. We'll find somebody to help us—as long as we keep clear of Dapper Dan and Helvitius."

The Weed pondered a while. "Kellytown. Not really civilization, but the nearest thing to it around here. I passed by it once. There's a livery stable. The blacksmith Dapper Dan claimed he was waiting for. A general store, a tavern for the locals. We might be able to hire a couple of horses, maybe a wagon."

"Kellytown it is," Vesper said. "We'll try it."

The Weed glanced up at the sky, purple once more with rain clouds. "A bit far to go before nightfall, and worse for the young ones if it's going to pour again. We can hole up now, rest, and get a good start in the morning."

The Weed recalled a pond no great distance away. He had, on occasion, ice-skated there. "It just might do."

I did not see that winter sport had any bearing on our need for shelter.

"But it does, sir," said The Weed. "I remember a little warming house. We used to sit inside to thaw our feet. Nice and snug—if it's still there."

Anything would be better than a wet night in the Aronimink undergrowth. We set off, then, Vesper and The Weed striding ahead, with Paulo dogging their footsteps and dividing his gaze of devotion between Vesper and The Weed, whose ear-wiggling must have made a deep impression on the youngster. Bringing up the rear, Smiler and Slider would have carried little Januaria. But the cherub insisted on riding on my shoulders, from which position she clutched my ears, nose, or hair whenever my steps faltered and she felt her balance threatened.

Thus jogging along, she happily burst into a kind of chant, much like those mysterious singsong rhymes that accompany rope-skipping or other inscrutable juvenile activities.

"Carla San Jeen," she piped. "Blonda Smitreen."

This incantation, after a time, produced an almost hypnotic effect on me. Despite myself, I hummed these nonsense syllables along with her. They floated in my mind even when we stopped for the occasional rest.

We reached the pond at dusk. The warming house still existed, though it was smaller than The Weed's recollection of it and much more ramshackle. Nevertheless, it offered shelter of sorts—and a welcome one, for the clouds burst a few moments after we crowded through the low doorway.

"Mongri," said little Januaria.

We were all hungry, I told her. Since she was small, I explained, her appetite was equally tiny. She did not accept my logic and refuted it in a word, "Waneet."

Blessedly, Smiler had possessed enough presence of mind in General Gallaway's kitchen to cram his pockets with bread and cheese, and we shared out these meager rations.

The children, by and large, bore their discomfort bravely. Paulo offered to stand watch along with his elders, but he was not too displeased when Vesper declined his offer. He curled up in a corner of the warming house, as did little Januaria. The poor angel sang herself to sleep with a few murmured repetitions of the now-familiar refrain, "Carla San Jeen, Blonda Smitreen"—and it had the same lulling effect on me.

By the time I woke, The Weed had already gone to Kellytown. He had left, Vesper told me, at the crack of dawn. The children, with the impatience of youth, fretted over his absence and restlessly awaited his return. By late morning, Vesper glimpsed The Weed rounding the pond. Her face fell. We had expected him to bring some sort of transportation. He was on foot.

"Better clear out," he said, as he hurried into the warming house. "Everybody in Kellytown's looking for us."

❧ 14 ❧

"On the bright side of it, sir," The Weed went on, seeing me start in alarm, "there aren't that many people in Kellytown."

"Enough to give us trouble," Vesper said. "What stirred them up?"

"Gallaway," said The Weed. "I stopped in the general store to buy some food"—he held out a small sack—"and never had a chance at the livery stable. At first, the storekeeper thought I'd come to join the search party.

"The way he told it, last night Gallaway and another man, a big, white-haired fellow—Helvitius, wouldn't you say?—came rounding up everybody they could find. Gallaway made quite a tale of it. He'd been attacked by a roving gang of cutthroats. They robbed him, assaulted his cook, and kidnapped his visiting niece and nephew. He's got them hopping mad at us."

It was inconceivable to me. The honest yeomanry of Kellytown would hardly be persuaded to turn themselves into bloodthirsty vigilantes.

"Helvitius paid them," said The Weed.

"That would do it," observed Vesper.

"Indeed it would, sir," put in Smiler. "You'd be surprised how people can turn disagreeable when they're paid to be."

"Spurs them on, as you might say," added Slider. "We've had a little experience with bounty hunters in our time. They're persistent."

"Yes, and there's a handsome reward for who gets us first," said The Weed. "The storekeeper didn't know if that meant dead or alive. I think he was already starting to get a little suspicious of me, so I didn't wait to find out. Not that it matters."

Whatever apprehension Vesper felt, she calmly and quickly got the children together and ready to travel. Januaria, still sleepy and fretful, was reluctant to leave the warming house, so again I hoisted the dear cherub onto my shoulders. Paulo, however, was bright and eager to be on the way, all in all taking our predicament as a new and exciting game. Young innocent, he had no notion of real danger. Peaceable by nature, our stalwart countryfolk can be aggressive when armed with pitchforks, clubs, and firearms. I would rather face a dozen Turkish bazaar ruffians than one aroused Kellytowner seeking profit.

Between them, Vesper and The Weed had decided that our best course lay straight northward through the Drexel Hills.

"Toby's been over the trails before," said Vesper. "It's not too bad. It won't be easy finding us in the hills. If we get through, we'll have a pretty clear run into Strafford. We'll have to keep off the roads, but at least we'll be out of Aronimink."

"Think of Xenophon, sir," The Weed suggested, "and the ten thousand Greeks he led across Asia Minor. Wasn't that a glorious moment when they sighted the Black Sea? *Thalatta, thalatta!* The sea, the sea! Good old Xenophon, he was something of a historian himself. A bit like you, sir, wouldn't you say?"

The Weed rattled on a while about the *Anabasis* and the famous march upcountry, as if he had been there. I suspected he would have relished outwitting the Persians. The Weed was developing a reckless streak that I found unsettling. That easy, loose-limbed gait of his reminded me of another neck-or-nothing hothead: Nilo, who could have lost us in the backlands of Illyria—and enjoyed it. The Weed, at least, did not spout old Illyrian proverbs.

With little Januaria clutching my ears and nose, I tried to keep up with the pace set by Vesper and The Weed. The twins jogged steadily. Young Paulo had fallen into step with his ear-wiggling hero, imitating his gangling stride. Januaria again piped up what had become her private anthem: "Carla San Jeen, Blonda Smitreen."

Out of irresistible curiosity, since the adorable angel could not answer my question, I called over Paulo and asked him what, for heaven's sake, she was repeatedly intoning. The boy shrugged. So I deduced that the refrain was not a Brazilian song or the names of some sorely missed playmates. She might have overheard General Gallaway talking with Sergeant Shote and garbled some bit of the conversation—the strange sounds of the language might have caught her fancy, or she could have made it up.

"She is sometimes a silly little *papagallo,* what you call

a 'parrot,' " said Paulo, with the Olympian air of an older brother. "Do not pay attention to her."

His advice was difficult to follow, for Januaria's childish babbling proved contagious. The Weed picked it up as if he had found a new and amusing toy and began chanting along with her, sometimes alternating what now became our marching song with occasional cries of *"Thalatta, thalatta!"*

It did inspirit us and, surprisingly, eased the rigors of hacking through the undergrowth, and by late afternoon, we plunged into the harsh embrace of the Drexel Hills.

Our majestic Alleghenies may surpass the Drexel Hills in altitude, but not in spitefulness. For that, they can only be compared to the ghastly Haggar Mountains of Jedera. Most of the Haggar is bleakly devoid of life. In the Drexel Hills, there is entirely too much of it, mainly in the form of malicious biting and stinging insects, including an especially savage wood louse, unique to the area, almost as big as my thumbnail. Even the bramble bushes and wild barberry seemed possessed of malevolent lives of their own, plucking at us with their sharp talons. We were in constant danger of twisting our ankles on stones thrusting up like dragon's teeth. Garter snakes the size of young anacondas slithered across our path. The day, at least, had turned fair and bright. A dubious blessing for, instead of being drenched, we were broiled.

Vesper can always find some benefit in adversity. She gestured toward the lower reaches of the hills.

"It's as rough going for the Kellytowners as it is for us. Toby thinks we might have outrun them."

I was not so sure. From time to time, we heard distant cries from the searchers below. Helvitius must have set a high price on our heads to inspire such doggedness. I hoped that nightfall would oblige them to break off the hunt. By then, we ourselves could go no farther.

Yet, I give The Weed all due credit. He was as competent in the Drexel Hills as that blue-skinned warrior An-Jalil had been in guiding us through the Haggar. There were even moments when The Weed's sunbaked features held a similar expression of remoteness while his eyes, like those of the Tawarik chieftain, scanned some invisible horizon. Fortunately—except for those fragments of "Sheridan's Ride" and "Evangeline"—The Weed refrained from quoting poetry at us.

Of more immediate use, he discovered a trapper's old cabin. Though it reeked of the ghosts of uncured pelts—mostly skunk—the children, like ourselves, were too exhausted to be anything but grateful. Like Vesper, The Weed possessed a remarkable ability to make himself at home wherever he happened to be. He shared out the food from his sack, wiggled his ears at the youngsters, and installed us as comfortably as possible. Given his familiarity with hotel managers, pawnbrokers, pretzel vendors, and river boatmen—not to mention President Grant—I would not have been too surprised if the phantom of the trapper himself had materialized to greet him with "Hello there, Toby."

Early next morning, we began our descent from the Drexel Hills. We had heard no sound of pursuit for several hours, and I let myself hope the Kellytowners had given up their search. With the Aronimink wilderness behind us, The Weed paused a moment to survey the gently rolling meadows below, the little clusters of woodlands, the seas of cultivated green fields.

"*Thalatta, thalatta!*" said The Weed.

"Blonda Smitreen," said little Januaria.

We hurried down the final slopes and into disaster.

Vesper had wisely decided, as a precaution, that we should keep off heavily traveled roads. A disheveled band of seven apparent vagabonds, including two grimy children, would have attracted unwanted attention. We could not guess what new villainy General Gallaway and Helvitius might undertake to lay hands on us. And so we followed Vesper's guidance until we reached the quiet precincts of Manoa. The strain of the past days had taken its toll on the youngsters. Januaria, her angelic face pinched and wan, had given up her marching song and whimpered on my shoulder. Paulo's taste for adventure, as well as his shoes, had worn thin. Vesper and The Weed could do nothing to cheer him. The sight of a smooth and empty lane, after hours of rutted byways, irresistibly tempted all of us.

The good folk of Manoa were at their Sunday devotions. At the pleadings of the footsore Paulo, Vesper agreed to follow this road and to leave it the moment we risked being observed. What a relief it was to step along easily, as we did for some quarter of a mile. Then Vesper halted. She motioned for us to turn aside. Ahead stood a white clapboard Quaker meeting house, a number of carriages and buggies tethered near the little burying ground.

Paulo's eyes lit up. Perhaps, in his weariness, the lad saw only a chance to ride instead of walk. Perhaps he itched to show off his enterprise and daring. In either case, before Vesper realized what he had in mind, Paulo was off like a shot, sprinting toward the nearest carriage: for the modest Quakers, a surprisingly elegant, shining new open-topped vehicle.

"Tubigawses." Januaria roused and brightened.

We sped after Paulo. He had already untethered the pair of horses and leaped into the carriage, shouting for us to join him.

Quaker meetings, in my opinion, last too long, or seem to. Now I wished the present one had lasted longer. For it was at that unlucky moment the services ended and the congregation emerged from the meeting house.

By then, Paulo had managed to turn the carriage onto the road. Another moment and the worshipers, to their consternation, understood that the vehicle had been commandeered by a ragged boy, whooping and slapping the reins, apparently aided by a ragtag band of desperate outlaws. They ran to apprehend us. Judging from their facial and vocal expressions, the usually gentle and tolerant members of the Society of Friends were highly displeased.

"We're in for it one way or another." Vesper, ordinarily, would never dream of making off with another's property. The opportunity, in this case, had been forced upon her. She chose, rightly or wrongly, to make the most of it. "Come on, Brinnie. Don't wait around."

Vesper jumped into the carriage, The Weed behind her. Objections useless at this point, I clambered in with little Januaria. Smiler and Slider took the reins from Paulo. The horses bolted down the lane.

Behind us, the congregation shouted and shook their fists. Some of the Friends had untethered their own carriages to set after us. I had never seen infuriated Quakers. I dreaded the consequences.

"The worst they'll do is reason with us," Vesper said as we sped along. "There"—she pointed—"that's what I don't like."

A police van had sighted us streaking through the sleepy town of Manoa. A runaway carriage alone would have been enough to draw attention. One careening vehicle followed by a string of others filled with gesticulating Friends could not go ignored. The van joined in hot pursuit.

"We are safe!" I exclaimed, urging Slider to halt. "Safe in the arms of the law!"

"Keep on!" cried Vesper. "Brinnie—if they catch us, how do we explain? What do we explain? The children? Dom Pedro's licenses? Sam Grant didn't want a word of this to the police or anyone else."

I saw her point. The guardians of the law were as much to be avoided as General Gallaway, Helvitius, and the Kellytowners. Not that we had any choice. Restricted to the sober, steady gait of their owners, the horses welcomed this unexpected liberation. Their blood was up, the bits were in their teeth. Not even the skillful Slider or Smiler could hold them back.

Rounding a turn on two wheels, the carriage and pair bulleted into the West Chester Pike, crashing through the toll gate and splintering it like matchwood. The hard-packed, empty road lay clear before us. The horses stretched to a gallop. The Quakers and police were hopelessly outdistanced as we plunged onward at breathtaking speed.

I resigned myself to the use of stolen property. As I

remarked to Vesper, we were making splendid progress at high speed along a good road.

"Only one problem," replied Vesper. "We're going in the wrong direction."

She clambered beside the twins to help them curb the mettlesome horses. By now, we were farther than ever from Strafford. The Quakers had given up the chase, but the police van reappeared in the distance, bearing down rapidly upon us. We tumbled from the carriage and into the woods.

Nothing is as demoralizing as being a fugitive in one's own habitat. It affected all of us. The Weed turned morose. The unflappable Smiler and Slider were glum and dispirited. The children fretted. Vesper maintained her customary optimism only with greatest difficulty. Without the dear girl's constant encouragement, even I might have lost heart altogether.

I prefer to pass over the rest of our weary way to Strafford. It was uneventful, unless all-encompassing misery may be counted an event. The Weed's provisions were soon exhausted. We spent the night huddled in a drainage ditch. Little Januaria declared "Wannafrup"—and did so upon my shoes. Paulo had a crying spell. No amount of ear-wiggling by The Weed consoled him. In short, what should have been a day's travel stretched to double that. In the trackless forests of Bryn Mawr and Haverford, I dreamed fondly of the El Dorado jungle and the burning sands of the Sahkra Desert.

Thanks to Vesper's often forceful urging, we pressed on. I lost all track of time; my watch had stopped long ago as a result of its immersion in the Schuylkill swamp. As best I could reckon, it was Tuesday midnight before we came to Strafford.

Until then, we had barely been able to set one foot in front of the other. The sight of the rambling house, lamps aglow in the windows, worked a miracle upon us. As if by unspoken agreement, by common inspiration, we threw off our exhaustion and began to run: slowly at first, then with joyous relief quickening our steps.

With Januaria crowing gleefully, we sped up the gracefully curving carriageway, past gardens and orchards, across the verandah and through the door. I called out for Mary. Light shone from the open library. Dear Mary, she had gone there to find comfort in solitude. We crowded into this quiet sanctuary.

Mary was not there.

"Welcome home," said Dr. Helvitius.

CHAPTER

❧ 15 ❧

"Where's Aunt Mary?" demanded Vesper.

Even with her life hanging by a thread, the dear girl has always kept her dignity and self-possession. At the sight of that archfiend in the very heart of these sacred precincts and bosom of our home, she came as close to losing those qualities as I had ever seen. Indeed, the nightmare vision of Helvitius at the library table, occupying my chair and with some of my papers spread around him so shocked me that I nearly overlooked the horrible significance of Mary's absence.

"If you have dared to harm so much as a hair—" I started forward, I would not have been accountable for my actions had I laid hands on the monster.

"Careful, sir," muttered The Weed, as Vesper put out a restraining arm. Only then did I notice the lantern-jawed Sergeant Shote lounging on the divan, his carbine across his knees. Beside him, armed with hunting rifles, stood two individuals with faces like slabs of raw beef, a malevolent pair of ruffians I had to assume were Kellytowners.

"Your good lady wife is not in residence at the moment," said Helvitius. "She was already absent when I arrived this morning. I regret missing the opportunity to pay her my respects. As for yourselves, your progress was observed by these gentlemen"—he nodded at the Kelly-towners—"and the excellent Sergeant Shote. I did not order them to hinder you. When I understood your destination, I felt it would be a more pleasant reunion if I were here to greet you."

Despite our own plight, relief flooded over me. Mary, at least, was safe. I guessed that she had, in her anxiety over us, returned to La Pierre House to consult with Dom Pedro.

"Without a hostess to receive me," Helvitius went on, inclining his head toward Vesper, "I took the liberty of making myself comfortable in your charming abode."

Wretch! He had not only scattered papers about and taken some volumes from the bookshelves, he had set a plate of chicken bones and an empty wine goblet on the latest pages of my Etruscan history.

"My intrusion will be brief," said Helvitius. "I am on my way to your Centennial Exposition. The opening ceremonies take place at noon tomorrow. I plan to attend. You, alas, will not be in a position to do likewise. I shall give you a detailed account. I guarantee it will be of exceptional interest. Before I depart, as I intend to be there well before the crowds, we have business to conclude."

Helvitius fixed his glance on The Weed. "You, I have been told, are the bearer of Dom Pedro's documents. Is that still the case?"

The Weed did not answer.

"I assume that it is," said Helvitius. He snapped his fingers. "I shall have those papers now."

The Weed gave his usual loopy grin, but his eyes had a dangerous glint. "If you want them, sir—well, you'll have to come and get them."

"As you please." Helvitius beckoned to Sergeant Shote and the Kellytown ruffians. The Weed straightened. The young idiot was undoubtedly contemplating something foolhardy.

"Toby, for heaven's sake," whispered Vesper, "hand them over."

"I don't like being told—"

"Well, I'm telling you," said Vesper.

"Oh," said The Weed. "That's different, then."

The Weed struck away the sergeant's searching hand and drew the papers from his jacket. While the Kellytowners removed the knives from the belts of Smiler and Slider, Sergeant Shote passed the documents to Helvitius, who carefully scanned them.

"The emperor has followed my instructions." Helvitius nodded with satisfaction. "You have read them, Miss Holly? Then you understand their value."

"Exactly," said Vesper.

"Once I complete my visit to the Centennial, I embark for Brazil," said Helvitius, "where I shall present these licenses to the imperial court."

"I'd like to see what happens when you do," said Vesper.

"Perhaps you shall," said Helvitius. "The children, of course, shall accompany me. I have no intention of giving them up. They may prove to be of further use. As for yourself, I have not yet decided. You have thwarted my plans too often before. It might please me for you to witness one enterprise you cannot hinder.

"The riches of Brazil will soon be in my hands. That, however, is a mere beginning. In time, I foresee an even greater position for myself. I shall direct the future of that great empire. The possibilities are limitless. The conquest of Paraguay, Argentina, all of South America—"

"You're expecting a lot from those papers," said Vesper, "especially since they're worthless. I'm surprised you don't know that."

"But I do, Miss Holly." Helvitius smiled. "I have never underestimated your intelligence. Do not underestimate mine. I know quite well that Dom Pedro can nullify the licenses. Princess Isabella will not. She will accept them as an official act of her father; she will have no reason to believe otherwise. Also, I count on my many secret supporters in the government of Brazil. They will urge her to carry out her father's wishes and will do so very eloquently, since they look forward to sharing in my profits. Isabella and her husband will be more than satisfied with their new ranks: empress and emperor.

"Perhaps, Miss Holly, you have begun to understand. Dom Pedro will not return from Philadelphia to Brazil. For the excellent reason that he, very shortly, will no longer exist."

"Assassin!" I cried. "So that is your murderous plan!"

"I wondered if you had something like that in mind," Vesper said, "but I couldn't believe you did. If anything happens to Dom Pedro, there's someone else who can tell Princess Isabella the truth about the whole business. I won't underestimate your intelligence. Even you must have thought of that."

"I have," replied Helvitius. "I presume you refer to your President Grant."

"He wanted to keep all this a secret," said Vesper. "He won't do it. Not if you harm Dom Pedro or any of us."

"You still do not grasp the magnitude of my enterprise," replied Helvitius. "Like Dom Pedro, President Grant will cease to exist. And so, alas, will Mrs. Grant, Empress Theresa, and half of your government's cabinet.

"The nation will reel in horror; the government itself will be in chaos. It stands already on the brink. This one event will suffice to topple it over.

"Do not be unduly alarmed," Helvitius went on. "A certain military individual will come forward to take a firm hand at the helm of the foundering ship of state. He is already on his way to Willard's Hotel in Washington City. He and a number of his like-minded brother officers await word from me. They will act vigorously and quickly. Order will be restored. A grateful public will be overjoyed to welcome this heroic personage as their leader."

"General Custer!" I exclaimed.

"No, Brinnie," murmured Vesper. "Gallaway. Dapper Dan."

"Precisely," said Helvitius.

"That maniac!" I burst out. "That madman!"

"Not so mad as all that," said Helvitius, "but enough to make an excellent public figure. He will rely completely on my advice and guidance. In time, at my recommendation, he will form a powerful alliance with Brazil.

That is to say, for all practical purposes, with me. Did I speak only of South America? Miss Holly, I envision a grand empire including Canada, Mexico, even El Dorado. The entire Western Hemisphere. Beyond that, who can say?"

Vesper fell silent at the revelation of this enormity. I, too, was horrified until I realized that Helvitius, in all his grandiose villainy, had overlooked the one thing that would destroy his diabolic scheme.

"You shall fail, sir," I flung at him. "You have forgotten that anchor, that bulwark of our Union: the Constitution! And still another tower of strength: the Congress of the United States!"

Helvitius gave me a pitying smile. "My dear Professor Garrett, your Constitution is a most admirable document. I doubt, however, that many of your fellow citizens have read it. They will, for the most part, care little whether it is observed or not. And a number of your congressmen would, I daresay, be delighted if that compendium of legalities vanished altogether."

Helvitius stood up. "You must excuse me now. Sergeant Shote and I have a few details to settle. I shall return as soon as possible. Before the day is out, you shall be comfortably aboard the *Minotaur*."

As Sergeant Shote and one of the Kellytowners left the library, Helvitius paused at the doorway.

"Professor Garrett, I took the opportunity to read a portion of your Etruscan history. Though I detected a number of errors, it is not entirely without a small degree of merit. I regret that you will be unable to finish it."

"Monster!" I cried. "Have you dared—?"

The door closed behind him. Despite this final outrage, my spirits actually rose a little. Whatever our personal fate might be, we no longer need fear for the safety of President Grant and Emperor Dom Pedro. Indeed, I realized, Helvitius's despicable scheme was nothing but self-delusion, pure lunacy, the disordered dream of a megalomaniac. He had, at last, overstepped the brink of sanity. I assured Vesper that his ravings had no foundation in reality. It was utterly impossible for him to dispose of the president, the emperor, their wives, let alone an array of dignitaries, all in one fell blow.

"Yes, he can," Vesper said. "I know how."

Vesper's powers of deductive reasoning and logical analysis are, of course, formidable. In this case, I saw no way her brilliant intellect could have reached such a conclusion.

"Brinnie, I know how he'll do it, and I know where he'll do it," said Vesper. "We all know. Little Januaria told us."

❧ 16 ❧

"We just weren't listening to her—"

Vesper broke off then. The Kellytowner had come back, bearing coils of rope; with him were a couple of sailors I recognized from the *Minotaur*'s crew. Helvitius must have invaded the house with more of his hirelings than I had supposed. Outnumbered as we were, Vesper understood the futility of resistance. The Weed struggled a little—no doubt it made him feel better—but he was quickly trussed up like the rest of us. Nor were Paulo and Januaria spared.

Vesper applied her most persuasive efforts to reason with our captors.

"Listen to me, you idiots," she remarked. "Do you think Helvitius is going to let you stay alive after he's through with you? And you"—she addressed one of the Kellytowners—"you heard what he's going to do. Dozens, hundreds of lives—"

"The Constitution itself, sir!" I exclaimed. "The very foundation of our Union!"

The big lout stared blankly. Had he paid no attention to Helvitius's words? Had their dreadful significance eluded him? Surely, Kellytown counted as part of the United States.

Unmoved by Vesper's appeal to his self-interest and mine to his patriotism, the yokel departed, as did his fellows, leaving us immobilized on the floor.

Few things in life are more disheartening than being bound hand and foot and made a helpless captive in the sanctity of one's own home. I tried to resign myself. Helvitius, at last, had triumphed. Equally painful, in a personal sense, had been that villain's comment on my Etruscan history. Compared with the wholesale destruction he had set out to inflict on Grant, Dom Pedro, and our entire government, it was, perhaps, of less importance. Still, no academic or literary person tolerates being damned with faint praise, and I confess I harbored a certain degree of irritation with that arrogant scoundrel.

Vesper's thoughts at this darkest hour had nevertheless turned toward freedom. No sooner left to ourselves than she began struggling against her bonds.

"Those fellows tie good knots," said Smiler, who had been doing likewise, with equal lack of success.

"As you'd expect from sailors," added the discouraged Slider.

"Can't one of us get loose?" Vesper cried. "If we could move that bookshelf—"

The Weed brightened. "That's it! The only way!"

Still chewing over my small annoyance with Helvitius's remarks about my Etruscan history, I did not at first understand Vesper's intention. Then my spirits rose. The hidden passageways, unused since the days when the mansion had proudly served as a station on the Underground Railroad! Too preoccupied with my quite justifiable vexation, I had forgotten them. The same corridors which aided escaping slaves would serve as our own road to liberty. An instant later, my hopes shattered. We were still bound hand and foot. We could never negotiate the narrow corridors.

"One thing at a time." Vesper had begun rolling across the carpet toward the book-lined wall. "If I can get that door open, we'll deal with the rest somehow."

Even as she spoke, I stared in bewilderment. A portion of the shelves had swung outward. There stood the most welcome sight I had ever seen.

"Aunt Mary!" cried Vesper.

"Ammari?" said little Januaria.

"Dearest rescuing angel!" I exclaimed. "Quickly! Lose not a moment!"

Mary's immediate attention, however, went to the children. "The poor darlings!"

She ran to Januaria and Paulo. Her delicate hands worked at the hard knots with a vigor I found astonishing. I had never seen the dear angel untangle anything more daunting than a skein of yarn.

"Helvitius told us you weren't here," said Vesper. "Where were you? How did you get back into the house?"

"His assumption was incorrect," replied Mary. "I did not get back into the house, dear child. I never left it. I saw that disgusting creature drive up with half a dozen crude individuals on horseback. It was too late for me to flee. I asked myself what my dear Brinnie would have

117

done. I could not imagine. So, the most practical course was to hide.

"I had time only to leave a note, saying I had gone by train to Philadelphia. Otherwise, that intolerable creature would have searched the house for me. I was obliged to remain in those dusty cubbyholes, most uncomfortably, while that band of ruffians made free of our pantry, our best china—"

I could not have been more proud of Mary's presence of mind, but I urged her to make haste.

"Do be patient, Brinnie. I shall attend to you directly." Mary had loosened the children's bonds and, giving them a consoling embrace, turned her efforts to freeing Vesper.

"We must all return to hiding," Mary went on. "I suggest, as well, opening the library casement. When that loathsome being comes back, he will believe you have escaped. We need only wait quietly. Sooner or later, he will go away."

"We can't wait," said Vesper, as she helped Mary untie the rest of us. "Did you hear him? The Exposition opens in a few hours."

"I suggest postponing our visit," said Mary. "The children must be taken to safety. We shall have ample opportunity to enjoy the exhibits in calmer circumstances. Dear Brinnie, for once, is correct: That monstrous creature cannot possibly carry out his threat."

"If we don't get to Fairmount Park right away, there won't be an Exposition," said Vesper. "Brinnie, that's what I started telling you. Helvitius has packed Machinery Hall with dynamite or something. Don't you see? That has to be his plan. When Sam and Dom Pedro turn the starting valve, the whole place will go sky-high."

"I think that's right, sir," put in The Weed. "There's no other way he can get rid of so many people all at once. Like the Gunpowder Plot, with Guy Fawkes trying to blow up the Houses of Parliament, wouldn't you say?"

My blood ran suddenly cold. Vesper had seen to the heart of a scheme so fiendish that all the past criminal endeavors of Helvitius turned trivial in comparison. She had come to the only possible conclusion; I knew that beyond question. I also knew, to my despair, we could not prevent it.

"We cannot reach the Exposition grounds before noon!" I cried in dismay. "There is no time!"

"We can," insisted Vesper. "Just barely, but we can do it. We have to, no matter what."

Wasting no more of our precious moments, Vesper darted into the passageway. Following Mary's excellent suggestion, Smiler and Slider flung open the casements. The Weed bolted the library door and hurried to join us. Mary had taken Januaria into her protective embrace, Paulo clung to her skirts. We groped our way along the lightless tunnel while Vesper sped on ahead. She had known these passages since childhood and could have gone through them blindfolded.

By the time we caught up with her, she had shouldered open a long-unused portal. We passed through it to find ourselves inside the carriage house and adjoining stables. Smiler and Slider immediately set about hitching up Hengist and Horsa. Before the steeds could greet Vesper with their usual whinny of recognition, The Weed ran to them, stroking their necks and murmuring in their ears. He could have been reciting Wordsworth or the *Farmer's Almanac* for all I knew, but the effect was astonishing. The horses calmed instantly, as if understanding our peril and the need for silence.

Mary and the children climbed into the open-topped carriage. The twins buckled the last harness leathers and sprang to the driver's bench. Vesper had already taken her place there and seized the reins. The Weed, on foot beside me, went cautiously to peer out a side window. He signaled our way was clear.

I flung open the doors of the carriage house and stared into the grinning face of Sergeant Shote.

❧ 17 ❧

The sight of his former captives, including the presumably absent Mary, not only free but springing out of nowhere, in possession of a vehicle and pair of horses, could not have failed to give Sergeant Shote cause for amazement. Yet, hardened soldier that he was, he took this turn of events in stride. Without hesitation, he raised his carbine and leveled it at his nearest target: myself.

When faced with a loaded gun, I have always exercised the utmost discretion and tactfulness. Yet, these had been severely trying days. My loved ones had been exposed to extreme danger; I had been half drowned in a fetid swamp, harried through the wilds of Aronimink and the Drexel Hills, pursued by indignant Quakers, and had my Etruscan history practically dismissed out of hand. In addition, horrible visions of Machinery Hall and those in attendance disintegrating in one shattering explosion roiled through my head. I mention these personal details only to convey my state of mind and my impatience at being frustrated at the very moment of our escape.

Against all the dictates of prudence, without reckoning the consequences of an action I normally would have disapproved as foolhardy, I seized the barrel of the weapon and bent every effort to wrest it from the hands of Sergeant Shote.

He fired; the blast from the muzzle scorched my face; the bullet, fortunately, buzzed past my ear. The shot rang through the carriage house. Hengist and Horsa reared in alarm.

"Boom-boom!" exclaimed little Januaria.

Vesper would have leaped to my assistance, but The Weed had already dashed up to grapple with Shote. I tried to maintain my grip on the barrel, which swung in all directions as Shote attempted to fling himself clear of The Weed.

That same instant, little Januaria wiggled from Mary's sheltering arms and nipped out of the carriage. Paulo sprang after her as the delightful cherub darted into the fray.

"Bamman!" Januaria remarked to Sergeant Shote. "Gway!"

Occupied though he was in fending off Paulo and The Weed, Shote tore the gun barrel from my hand. Before he could fire again, Januaria found access to his shins and kicked them with even more vigor than she had once applied to mine.

Cursing, yelping with sudden pain inflicted by this miniature tornado, Shote lost both his balance and his hold on the weapon. He went sprawling to the ground, the carbine spun from his hands. Paulo would have run to snatch it up, but Hengist and Horsa plunged through the open doors. I barely had time to seize little Januaria and scramble aboard, Paulo and The Weed tumbling headlong after us.

The gunfire, in addition to Shote's outcries, brought the other ruffians from the house. By then, however, Hengist and Horsa were bolting down the carriageway.

Vesper was standing like a marmalade-haired charioteer and whistling through her teeth. The carriage lurched down the road. Hengist and Horsa laid back their ears and stretched into a gallop.

"We've done for them!" The Weed's face was alight, he waved his arms in joyful triumph. Had I not pulled him back, I sincerely believe that, in his exuberance, he would have climbed astride one of the horses.

"We've got the distance on them now." He turned a bright grin upon me. "Ghent to Aix, sir, wouldn't you say?"

For a moment, I did not comprehend him.

"Why, it's Browning, sir. 'How They Brought the Good News from Ghent to Aix': 'I sprang to the stirrup, and Joris, and he; I gallop'd, Dirck gallop'd, we gallop'd all three.' Hard to sort out who's doing all the galloping, but it doesn't matter. They got to Aix— Odd, though, isn't it? Nobody says what the good news was. It must have been marvelous, even so."

I clapped my hands to my head as The Weed babbled on. He was correct in one thing, at least. By the time Shote and his band saddled their horses, we would have thoroughly outdistanced them. For the first time, I began to believe in our chances, however slim, of reaching Fairmount Park and the Exposition grounds.

Vesper was certain of it. She felt confident enough to slow our pace a little—wisely so, though Hengist and Horsa would have burst their gallant hearts if she required it of them. She chose instead to husband their strength for the many miles ahead.

Nevertheless, we continued steadily and swiftly. The sun had risen pale white in a hazy sky; a warm drizzle fell upon us, but we tolerated it rather than stopping to raise the carriage top. Vesper had chosen to avoid such busy thoroughfares as the Lancaster Turnpike, and we clattered along the misty lanes, past occasional farmhouses and cottages.

Mary held the children close, as the wind whistled in our ears and grew ever louder. Our pace, brisk though it was, did not justify such a sound. I caught my breath. It was not the wind.

Through a break in the trees lining our course, I glimpsed a plume of smoke. The whistle shrieked again. To my dismay, I realized we were bearing toward a rail crossing, a locomotive of our efficient Pennsylvania Railroad speeding along the tracks.

Vesper urged the horses onward, hoping to cross in time. All the strength of Hengist and Horsa did not suffice. The train reached the crossing seconds before we did. Vesper could only rein in the steeds.

The cars jolted over the tracks in an endless line of impossible obstacles. The Weed shook his fists in frustration. Behind the locomotive rumbled freight cars, flatcars, passenger cars, the longest assemblage of rolling stock I had ever observed. From the windows, blissfully ignorant of the catastrophe looming over all the Western Hemisphere, the passengers waved and smiled at us; some of them were even eating breakfast.

Vesper sat grimly silent. The Weed fumed; I thought I would go mad with impatience. Little Januaria glanced back over Mary's shoulder.

"Awses," she declared.

CHAPTER

❧ 18 ❧

All of us heard the approaching hoofbeats. The Pennsylvania Railroad, of course, is the finest system of transportation in the world. I cursed it. The train had robbed us of time never to be recaptured.

Vesper, even so, remained undaunted. As the last car and the trailing caboose rattled past the crossing, she snatched the reins and sent Hengist and Horsa racing onward.

"Ghent to Aix!" cried The Weed. "We'll do it, sir!"

I dared not calculate how narrowly we skimmed the trees and bushes that sprang at us as Vesper drove our lurching vehicle down byways and across open fields, attempting to recover our advantage.

I soon understood that she was heading east, hoping to gain speed on the smooth road along the banks of the Schuylkill. From there, it would be a straight, swift run to the precincts of the park. I can give no details on how she reached this thoroughfare. I kept my eyes shut during most of our headlong progress.

I wish I could have shut my ears as well. The Weed kept on declaiming Browning's endlessly jogging versification: to the delight of Januaria, who clapped her hands in rhythm, and to my despair. I could overlook his Gond meditations, his lentils and beans, his Xenophon, everything but his taste in poetry.

To my astonishment, rather than increasing speed as we reached the west bank of the Schuylkill, Vesper pulled off the road. She sprang down, calling for Slider and Smiler to unhitch the horses.

"We'll ride Hengist and Horsa the rest of the way," said Vesper. "They'll go faster if they aren't pulling the carriage." When I pointed out that we had only two mounts, she added, "We're splitting up. Shote can't catch all of us. Aunt Mary, Januaria and Paulo had best find a place to hide. I don't want the children anywhere near Machinery Hall if the engine really does explode. Twins—"

"We'll make our own way to the Exposition," said Smiler. "No need to worry about us."

"We'll do whatever needs doing," added Slider.

The Weed had started toward Hengist. Vesper drew him back. "Toby, stay with Aunt Mary and the children. Keep them safe at all costs."

"Dear girl," I protested, as she prepared to mount Horsa, "you cannot think of galloping alone into some blazing inferno."

"No blazing inferno if I can help it," replied Vesper. "Alone?" she gently added. "I'll be with my dear old Brinnie."

We lost no time in fond farewells. Before little Januaria understood we were departing, we had already mounted. With the adorable cherub's tearful cry of "On-cabinni" ringing in my ears, we galloped up from the riverside into the rolling woodlands of Fairmount Park.

Shote and his ruffians had either given up the chase or had run afoul of Smiler and Slider. I heard no sounds of pursuit. Hengist and Horsa, their mouths foam-flecked, never slackened their gait. For a brief moment, I allowed myself to hope that our last effort would not be in vain.

We burst from the greenery of the park. The Exposition grounds came into view. The clouds had parted; the drizzle momentarily ceased. Ahead rose the lofty towers gilded in a shaft of sunlight, the dazzling glass domes, the banners proudly flying from the peaks of the magnificent structures. Vesper pulled up sharply. My heart sank.

We had failed.

Even Vesper's brilliant intellect had not taken into account this final obstacle. The main entrance, as well as most of the avenue itself, was packed. It was as if every citizen of Philadelphia had chosen to attend the opening ceremonies. We could not so much as approach let alone enter the gates of the doomed Exposition.

Vesper caught her breath at the sight, and I believe the dear girl herself gave way to despair if only for a moment.

"All right," she said, "we can't go by the front, we'll go by the back."

She clicked her tongue at Horsa. We made our way as quickly as our steeds could carry us from the crowded avenue and skirted the Exposition grounds. Vesper pointed ahead. The construction of iron fencing remained unfinished. Only a wooden barrier stood in the way of those few unpatriotic individuals who might have sought to gain entry without paying the modest fee of fifty cents. With a word of encouragement to Horsa, Vesper made straight for the barrier. I charged beside her. Our faithful mounts sailed over with inches to spare.

We cantered down a flower-lined pathway to an area of machine shops and service buildings adjoining Machinery Hall. Vesper dismounted and tethered our animals near an open shed. We strode toward a side entrance of the long, high-roofed structure. Vesper's pace was resolute but almost leisurely. I begged her to make haste. She turned a glance of radiant confidence upon me.

"Dear Brinnie," she said, "didn't you see the clock at the train station? We're way ahead of time."

Even as my hope sprang again to life, from the Grand Plaza rose bloodcurdling shrieks and dreadful wailing. I stopped short, horrified. Some new disaster, beyond the diabolic scheme of Helvitius, had fallen upon the spectators.

"The 'Centennial Hymn,'" said Vesper. "Never mind it. Just get a move on, Brinnie."

Machinery Hall lay deserted. The exhibitors had joined the throng at the Grand Plaza, where the world-renowned orchestra of Mr. Theodore Thomas made every effort to submerge the thousand-voice choir bellowing John Greenleaf Whittier's inspirational verses. We hurried along the empty aisles, paying no heed to the marvels of inventiveness on display. Near the front entrance, in solitary grandeur, stood the mighty engine itself.

Vesper ran ahead to the platform on which it reposed. I could only pause, wonder struck, before the awesome achievement of that self-taught engineering genius,

George Henry Corliss. Side by side, its massive cylinders soared like twin Gothic towers toward the vaulted ceiling. A framework of titanic girders supported a flywheel that must have been no less than thirty feet in diameter and perhaps three-score tons in weight. The idea that Helvitius had chosen this marvel of our modern world as an instrument of devastation turned my emotions from contemplative admiration to cold outrage.

"Brinnie, stop gawking," Vesper suggested. "Come help."

She had bent to examine the metal plates around the flooring of the engine. "Helvitius couldn't have put dynamite in the cylinders. It has to be underneath. Let's have a look."

Between us, we succeeded in heaving up one of the plates. Vesper lowered herself into the crawl space that now lay open.

"Can't see too well," she called back. "Wait—yes! The whole place is loaded with dynamite. It's a regular ammunition depot down here."

I advised her to come out promptly.

"No danger," said Vesper. "It can't go off until the engine starts. I have to find out how Helvitius rigged it."

I started to climb down. Vesper ordered me to stay aboveground; there was little enough room for her alone. I heard her scuffling around in the crawl space and muttering to herself. Outside, chorus and orchestra approached the triumphant climax of the "Centennial Hymn."

Vesper's head popped up. "He wired detonators to the pistons. I unwired them. Simple. Any halfway decent electrical engineer could do it."

I breathed a prayer of thanks that Vesper had devoted time in her laboratory experimenting with electricity, a subject I had, heretofore, considered impractical.

"Dear girl," I asked, "are you absolutely sure it's safe?"

"No," said Vesper. "Not yet. There's one more connection. Only it isn't down here."

She hoisted herself out and peered at the colossal cylinders. "There? It must be."

She ran to one of the iron ladders and clambered up. It made me dizzy to watch her as she swung onto a catwalk at the pinnacle of the towering engine.

From the Grand Plaza came still more earsplitting noises, a din of kettledrums and trumpets. Having dispatched the "Centennial Hymn," the orchestra was attacking the "Grand Centennial March" by the notorious Herr Richard Wagner. I could not help feeling a painful twinge of disapproval at the choice of this individual over one of our brilliant but respectable Philadelphia composers.

Vesper was still aloft when the dignitaries began to enter Machinery Hall. Empress Theresa on his arm, President Grant led the way. His eyes went to the mighty engine and his jaw dropped. Vesper leaned over the railing of the catwalk and waved at him.

"Hello there, Sam."

The astonished Grant left the side of the empress and hurried to the platform. Dom Pedro, escorting Mrs. Grant, stared an instant and followed him.

Vesper, meantime, had scuttled down the ladder. "The children are safe." She gestured toward the huge machine. "So's that."

She hastily told Grant and the emperor the most important details of Helvitius's scheme. Dom Pedro's eyes blazed with outrage. As Grant learned of General Gallaway's treachery, a bitter smile spread over his face.

"So Dapper Dan thought he'd take my place?" Grant muttered. "It would have served him right."

"Miss Holly, I cannot praise you sufficiently," said Dom Pedro. He turned to Grant. "In view of what this remarkable young woman has related, we dare not continue the opening ceremonies. The dynamite charges remain in place."

"No, sir," Grant replied. "I won't delay another moment. If Miss Vesper Holly says the United States, the Empire of Brazil, and this contraption here are all in good working order—well, sir, I'll take her word for it."

"I shall be honored to follow your example," said Dom Pedro.

As the expectant audience crowded around the platform, President Grant and Emperor Dom Pedro stepped toward the engine and turned the starting valve.

Explosions rocked Machinery Hall.

CHAPTER

❧ 19 ❧

My first thought was to fling my arms around Vesper, to shield her as best I could from the devastation sure to rain down upon our heads the next moment. Fortunately, I had no time to follow this protective impulse. The explosion came from the audience.

Cheers, applause, shouts of wonder rang through Machinery Hall as the gigantic flywheel began to turn, the mighty pistons plunged up and down, and power surged to all the other engines on display, which commenced rattling, whirring, and hissing out billows of steam. That same instant, bells pealed and festive cannon roared from nearby George's Hill. The choir of a thousand voices broke into Mr. Sidney Lanier's stirring "Meditation of Columbia." The orchestra persisted in Herr Wagner's grand march.

Caught up in the mass of dignitaries swarming up on the platform to congratulate Grant and Dom Pedro, we did not at first hear the urgent cries from Slider as he shouldered his way toward us.

"Helvitius!" he shouted in Vesper's ear. "Spotted him! Statue of Liberty!"

Vesper broke away from the throng of well-wishers. With Slider urging us to make all haste, we battled our way from Machinery Hall to the Grand Plaza. Once clear of the worst of the crowd, we raced across the broad Avenue of the Republic. I tried to learn the whereabouts of my dear Mary and the children. Wagner's music must have deafened me; the best I could understand from Slider's breathless reply was that they were safe in the hands of the navy.

"At sea?" I exclaimed.

"Not the U.S. Navy," said Slider. "The Schuylkill Navy."

I sought no further explanation, accepting that Mary, her young charges, and Tobias, as well, were out of danger. At Slider's direction, we ran toward the expanse of an artificial lake.

There, by the shore, as if some colossal being had started bursting from the earth, uplifting a torch in its mighty hand, rose the arm of the Statue of Liberty.

"He was there!" Smiler, awaiting us at the souvenir pavilion at the elbow of Liberty, pointed upward. Just below the sculptured flame, an ornamental ring formed a sort of balcony. This, I realized, was the vantage point Helvitius had chosen to observe the culmination of his monstrous conspiracy. Of the villain himself, there was no sign. Witnessing the failure of his scheme, seeing Machinery Hall still intact, he had climbed down the arm's interior ladder and fled the scene of his defeat.

"Gone?" cried Vesper, in anger and dismay. "No! I see him!"

Her keen eyes had glimpsed an unmistakable figure briskly proceeding down Fountain Avenue toward Horticultural Hall and the river a little distance beyond.

"The wretch!" I burst out. "He has escaped us again!"

Vesper would have raced after him on foot, but Smiler caught her arm. "We borrowed this to get here. You take it. Quicker than running."

He indicated a tandem bicycle leaning against the pavilion wall. Vesper's eyes lit up.

"Jump on, Brinnie!"

She sprang to the forward saddle and gripped the handlebars. I barely had the chance to climb astride behind her. She launched this two-seated vehicle into motion.

"Pedal for all you're worth!"

With Vesper steering the tandem and her long legs pumping vigorously, we sped down the avenue. Our swift conveyance rapidly closed the distance between us and Helvitius. Perhaps the shouts from the pedestrians scattering out of our path, or perhaps some bestial instinct—surely not his conscience—caused him to glance backwards. Seeing the tandem bearing down upon him, Helvitius broke into a run. We pedaled onward, drawing ever closer.

Then, as if any further proof of his ruthlessness were needed, Helvitius sighted a young lad innocently propelling himself on a penny-farthing bicycle, seized him by the collar, and flung him to the ground.

The despicable fiend swung onto the narrow seat above the high front wheel. The small rear wheel spun to a blur as he spurted ahead of us. I called to the passersby, urging them to halt the escaping villain, but they looked on our pursuit as one of the Centennial's sporting events and only waved their souvenir flags, cheering us on.

Helvitius streaked across Lansdowne Drive and down the pathway to the river. At first, I thought his goal was to lose himself in the dense forests of Manayunk. Then I glimpsed the *Minotaur*'s steam launch moored by one of the old footbridges. Once aboard the launch, his escape was certain.

The wind whistled in my ears as Vesper pedaled faster. The front of our tandem edged closer to the penny-farthing. In a burst of speed, Vesper drew nearly abreast of Helvitius. She turned the handlebars sharply. Her deliberate collision sent both bicycles out of control, flinging all of us to the ground.

Roaring with fury, Helvitius sprang to his feet. He tried to gain the riverside and the waiting launch. Vesper barred his way. She seized him, but he threw her aside and raced to the bridge. Gasping for the breath that had been knocked out of me, I disentangled myself from the tandem and ran to aid her.

In midspan, Vesper caught up to the fleeing Helvitius and grappled with him. He struck at her and sought again to tear himself away. With all the strength of his considerable bulk, he battered her against the wooden railing. Vesper clung doggedly to him. At the impact of the struggling pair, the railing shattered. With Vesper still locked in his hostile embrace, they hurtled through the air and pitched into the river below.

Urging Vesper to hold on, I dove headlong into the water. I struck out for the middle of the stream where the dear girl and Helvitius continued their combat.

Laboring for breath, I swam toward them. To my horror, they disappeared below the surface. Neither of them emerged.

At the same time, I heard a shout from downstream. In that instant, I understood Slider's hasty reference to the Schuylkill Navy. Speeding upriver came Philadelphia's boating enthusiasts and what seemed a whole flag-bedecked regatta of racing craft. In one sleek shell propelled by muscular oarsmen in athletic jerseys sat Mary and the children. Leading the fleet in a single scull, rowing with all his strength, was The Weed.

Oars flailing, he drew closer to me. I pointed to the spot where Vesper and Helvitius had vanished.

The Weed pulled alongside of me. I tried to swim clear, but as his single scull passed over me, the blade of an oar struck me full force on the head. The waters of the Schuylkill drowned my last anguished cry to Vesper. The river swallowed me into its lightless depths.

CHAPTER

❧ 20 ❧

Having resigned myself to a permanent resting place on the bed of the Schuylkill River, unconscious of any events taking place after that sickening moment when Vesper and Helvitius vanished and The Weed belabored my cranium with his oar, I opened my eyes. The Weed was peering anxiously at me.

"Come around at last, sir? You had us worried. Sorry for the accident."

As best I could tell, without much caring why or how, I was in our suite at La Pierre House. In the shaded lamplight, President Grant and Emperor Dom Pedro stood gravely watching at my bedside. And my dear Mary. One other face was absent. I started up, looking around wildly. Had Vesper escaped unharmed from all our other perils— only to be borne to the river bottom in the fatal clutches of Helvitius?

Then I felt that gentle, familiar hand on my brow. "Dear girl! You are not drowned!"

"Not quite," said Vesper. "Toby fished me out. You, too."

No doubt I should have been more effusive, but my head was going in circles as a result of The Weed's oarsmanship, and I was in no state to express eloquent gratitude. Yet, he had saved Vesper's life, mine as well, and in fact, I felt kindly disposed toward him.

The Weed waved aside my mumbled thanks. He was rather apologetic about the incident.

"Couldn't find Helvitius," he said. "After I pulled the two of you out, I went back a few times looking for him. Well, bad luck, sir, that is, for him."

"Last I saw him he was at the bottom of the Schuylkill," said Vesper. "The Schuylkill Navy dragged the river up and down. They didn't find him."

"What a helpful group of fine-looking young men," put in Mary. "Without them, we would still be at the Zoological Garden."

"The zoo?" My head spun all the more. What, for heaven's sake, was my dear Mary doing visiting the zoo?

"Quite a lovely setting," said Mary. "The twins found a bicycle there, the owners kindly loaned it to them. Tobias thought it would be the safest place for us, among the wild animals. And so it would have been, if that disagreeable Sergeant Shote had not found us. To his regret, I am happy to say. While he was attempting to shoot Tobias, I pushed him into the bear pit."

"You caused him to be devoured? You? Dear Mary—"

"There were no bears in residence," Mary replied.

139

"The attendants took him into custody. After that, Tobias obtained the help of those splendid boatmen."

"Yes, well, actually it was Max Schmitt," put in The Weed. "I used to row with him. Fine chap. Tom Eakins painted his picture, you know. He got the rest of the fellows to lend a hand."

"They've given up the search," said President Grant. "If he's alive, Helvitius won't get far. I telegraphed the Naval Station. They seized that fancy yacht of his. So, unless he's at the bottom of the river, he's on the run. We'll catch him sooner or later."

I did not share Grant's confidence. He did not know Helvitius as well as we did.

"Don't worry," Vesper said to me. "Senhora Da Costa's missing, too. My guess is she'll be looking for him with blood in her eye and a score to settle. If she finds him, he'll wish he were back in the Schuylkill."

"Now that I see you're all in one piece," Grant said, "I'll be on my way to Washington City. I want to hand out some new assignments to those officers who threw in with Dapper Dan. I'd like to court-martial every one of them, but I don't want any testimony on record. As I reminded this brave young lady, the whole affair has to stay a secret. Otherwise, my enemies could still discredit the government. If Dan's cronies don't keep their mouths shut, they'll be permanent latrine diggers out in the Territories."

"And General Gallaway?" I asked. "Will he go unpunished?"

"If Dapper Dan has any sense," replied Grant, "he'll light out for Mexico, beyond my reach. I don't expect he'll find much joy amid the cactus and scorpions."

I reminded Grant that the Kellytowners might have some inkling of the plot and were likely to talk about it.

Grant shrugged. "Let them. From what I've heard of the place, who's going to believe anybody from Aronimink?"

The president thanked all of us again and took the most admiring leave of Vesper. Dom Pedro accompanied him to the door, then returned to my bedside.

"We sail for Brazil at the end of the week," he said, "but I urge all of you to remain here as my guests until you are fully recuperated. Tomorrow, Miss Holly is doing me the honor of accompanying me to the Exposition. She has expressed an interest in meeting that friend of mine, young Aleck Bell. She may be able to give him some advice in perfecting his invention. Poor fellow, his display has been relegated to an obscure corner of the hall. I shall take it on myself to call attention to it, so that it will not go unnoticed.

"What a loss if such remarkable devices had been destroyed along with their inventors," Dom Pedro went on. "I confess I felt a little uneasy when the president and I turned the Corliss valve, even though Miss Holly assured us it was safe."

"I wasn't worried," said Vesper. "It was a lot of dynamite, though. By the way, Brinnie, we found out how Helvitius got it into Machinery Hall. He had some forged papers making him out to be a safety inspector, so he had free run of the place. He brought in the explosives little by little. That's what kept delaying the opening. Smiler and Slider are up there now, taking it all out. Sam ordered Machinery Hall closed temporarily. No visitors, no other workmen. Nobody will ever know it was there in the first place."

"Miss Holly has even retrieved my documents, and I have already destroyed them," said Dom Pedro. "Although they could not be enforced if I nullified them, I did not want them to fall accidentally into the wrong hands."

"Neither did I," said Vesper. "While Helvitius was trying to drown me, I picked his pocket. He was too busy to notice."

"Oncabinni!"

A joyful cry from the adorable cherub interrupted her. Empress Theresa had come into the chamber with Paulo and Januaria. The youngsters looked much cleaner than when I last saw them. Paulo shook my hand with gentlemanly courtesy. Little Januaria crawled onto my chest and affectionately squeezed my nose.

"She's the one we should all thank," said Vesper. "If she hadn't put me onto the scheme, I don't like to think what would have happened. I didn't have time to explain, but Januaria was telling us all along. She just didn't realize it. What she overheard—"

"Carla San Jeen!" Januaria gleefully cried. "Blonda Smitreen!"

The angel's gibberish still made no sense to me.

"Listen to her," said Vesper. "I should have understood it sooner than I did. 'Carla San Jeen'—Brinnie, what she's been saying is 'Corliss engine.' And 'Blonda Smitreen'—'blown to smithereens.' "

"Boom-boom-boom," remarked the cherub.

❧ 21 ❧

Despite the emperor's generous invitation, we did not remain long in the city. After the twins finished their work of removing the dynamite, and Vesper had toured the Exposition, I begged to return home. Though I had not yet entirely recovered, I was anxious to inspect my Etruscan history after its disrespectful handling by Helvitius.

When we took our leave of the imperial party, Dom Pedro and Empress Theresa repeating their deepest gratitude, there was a measure of tearfulness, which I always find disconcerting. Paulo unsuccessfully tried to conceal his trembling lips, and little Januaria sobbed wretchedly. Dear Mary sniffled and dabbed her eyes; the gentle soul had so quickly grown attached to the youngsters. I confess, too, that when Januaria flung her cherubic arms around my neck and had to be firmly peeled off, I blew my nose at frequent intervals.

In Strafford, the damage turned out less than I feared. The invading ruffians had broken much of the china and plundered all of the larder. But except for the chicken bones and the wet glass on my papers, my long unfinished work was intact.

During the days that followed, I saw little of The Weed or, for that matter, of Vesper and Mary. I was, however, aware that they were engaged in long conversations among themselves. Had I been of a suspicious turn of mind, I might have supposed they were up to something.

In fact, they were. One afternoon, Vesper and Mary came into the library. The Weed trailed along behind them.

"Toby has marvelous news," Vesper began.

"That's right, sir," The Weed confirmed. "What it is— well, I'm going back to Crete in a few days."

"My dear Tobias!" I sprang to my feet and joyfully shook his hand. "Marvelous news indeed!"

"I'm sure I'm right about my translation," said The Weed. "Definitely beans. Now I want a look at the rest of those inscriptions."

"Some other marvelous news, too," said Vesper. "I'm going with him."

I was too stunned to speak. Vesper leaving us? What thoughts crowded my mind in that instant: the dear girl's sun-blistered face during our crossing of the Haggar, her carefree laughter as we waltzed at Duchess Mitzi's diamond jubilee, our galloping through the Illyrian backlands, swimming the Culebra. And, with all that, my memory of La Pierre House, Vesper in her red caftan, my terrible fear that I was seeing her for the last time. I had been correct, though in a way I had never imagined.

"Dear girl," I finally murmured, "if that is your wish, then so you shall."

"Not unchaperoned," Mary quickly put in. "Indeed not." She paused a moment, then added, "That, my dear Brinnie, is why we are accompanying them.

"I shall enjoy observing the palace at Knossos," Mary continued. "And, having gone that far, it will be a rewarding experience to travel on to Constantinople, Baghdad, Bombay—"

I could not believe my ears. My gentle, delicate Mary amid foul-smelling bazaars and snake charmers? I felt obliged to express my firm opinion: It was utterly ridiculous, dangerous, and foolhardy.

"I knew you'd like the idea," said Vesper.

AUTHOR'S NOTE

For these past few years, Miss Vesper Holly has adventured in imaginary places that seem real. Now she adventures in a real place that seems imaginary, even fantastic: Philadelphia. Readers may well ask: How much is fact, how much is fiction?

Philadelphia, my birthplace and a city I dearly love, is a fact. So is 1876. In the backwash of the Civil War, our Centennial year was one of upset and unrest, marked by a rash of scandals; a brutal and disastrous Indian policy; and by one of the strangest and most conflicted elections in our history, stirring fears of rioting and armed insurrection.

The Centennial Exposition in Fairmount Park was as here depicted. The arm and torch of the Statue of Liberty were, in fact, displayed. The mighty Corliss engine was the wonder of the age. Richard Wagner did write the "Grand Centennial March," though musicologists judge it to be far from his best work—seldom played, but real nevertheless.

Vesper and Brinnie meet a number of historical figures. For one, President Grant. Though his family called him "Lyss," at West Point he acquired the nickname "Sam." Only his close friends and comrades-in-arms enjoyed the privilege of using that nickname. His allowing Vesper to do so represents quite an honor. At the Exposition's opening, Grant and the emperor of Brazil actually did start up the Corliss engine.

The emperor of Brazil may sound like somebody out of a fairy tale, but he is historically accurate. Dom Pedro II was a most enlightened sovereign, keenly interested in science and education. He became friends with Alexander Graham Bell while visiting Boston's City School for the Deaf, where Bell was working on new methods of teaching speech. At the Centennial, as a young unknown with a dubious invention, Bell was relegated to an obscure corner. Dom Pedro, one of the exhibition judges, sought him out and called enthusiastic attention to the new-fangled device. "It talks! It talks!" exclaimed Dom Pedro. Without that imperial endorsement, we might not have had the telephone.

Max Schmitt, the oarsman, has been immortalized in the famous painting by Philadelphia's Thomas Eakins. The Centennial rejected one of Eakins's masterpieces, *The Gross Clinic,* permitting its display only in the medical section, amid wooden legs, trusses, and patented ear cleaners. Generally ignored during his lifetime, Eakins is now recognized as one of America's great artists. He is definitely real.

On the other hand, the flamboyant and deranged General Daniel "Dapper Dan" Gallaway is definitely fictitious.

Even so, he closely resembles a real general: George Armstrong Custer. They are brothers under the skin. Like his fictional counterpart, Custer cherished political aspirations. In the Centennial summer of 1876, he hoped to advance his career by a triumph at Little Big Horn.

La Pierre House existed and was one of Philadelphia's most luxurious hotels. The infamous Pepper Pot Tavern is imaginary. Pepper pot soup, however, is an authentic Philadelphia specialty. So are soft pretzels, properly eaten with an application of mustard.

While distances are occasionally flexible, to suit the author's purposes, the localities are real: Haverford, Bryn Mawr, Manoa, Manayunk, and Strafford. My wife, daughter, and I lived in Kellytown in our first house. Always warmhearted and generous neighbors, the Kellytowners will, I know, forgive me for poking a little affectionate fun at them.

Is the savage wilderness of Aronimink real? No—and yes. I grew up there and its depiction matches my earliest recollections. My trusty companions and I constantly explored this vast forest primeval. Threatened with starvation, we ate wild blackberries. Risking life and limb, we swam the raging torrent of Darby Creek and plunged to its very depths of about three feet. The rocks of Indian Basin towered high above us. The Aronimink described is the Aronimink of my childhood imagination.

The same applies to the terrible hills of Drexel, which are hardly much above sea level. Winters, I sledded down their breakneck slopes. A summer mountaineer, my mother's clothesline coiled around my shoulder, I scaled their peaks: Everest and the Matterhorn combined. The geography of the imagination is always true.

Although it does not figure in this adventure, the Free Library of Philadelphia, with its excellent map collection, is real. So are my thanks for its gracious help in my research.

Drexel Hill,   —LLOYD ALEXANDER
Pennsylvania